By

STONE MARSHALL

Contributions by Nabru Marshall

Illustrations by Abraham Mast

Edited by Joni Wilson

Copyright © Stone Marshall, 2015
StoneMarshall.com
edition 2.0 January 2015
Published by Stone Marshall Publishing
ISBN-13:
978-1505898422
ISBN-10:
1505898420

Dedication

To Nabru, for enthusiastic contributions to Flynn's continuing story.

To the fans of Flynn's Log, thank you for your kind words and encouragement.

To my dear Karissa for your enduring support and comforting kisses.

FLYNN'S LOG 2, THORN'S LAIR

MAP OF THE DARK REALM

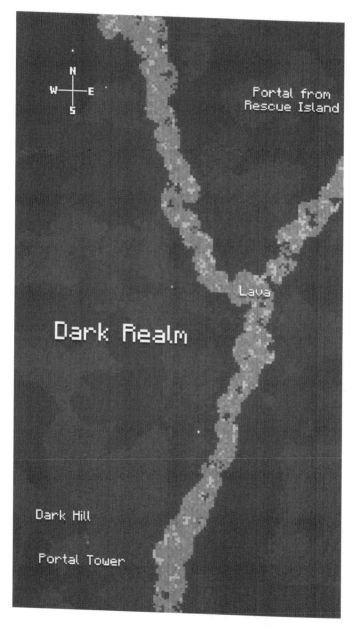

MAP OF ARCADE VILLAGE

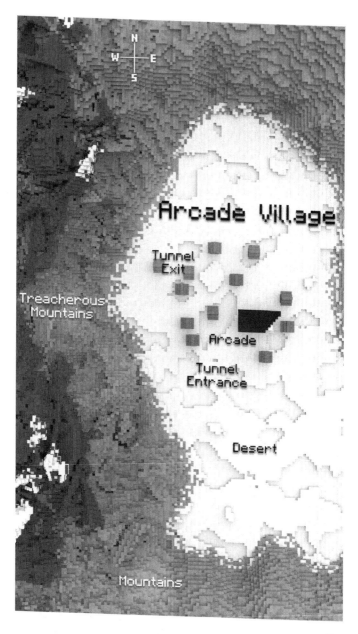

MAP OF TREACHEROUS MOUNTAINS

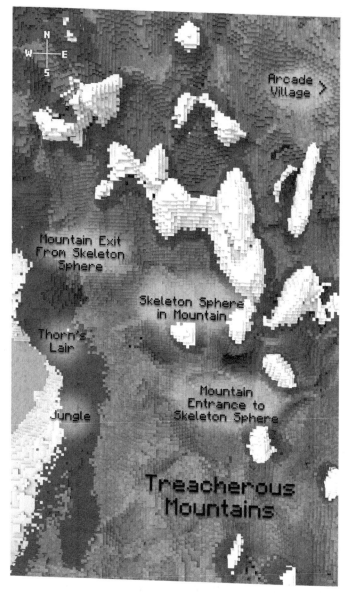

LOG ENTRY 1

The Portal

THERE IS A FIRST TIME FOR EVERYTHING. This is my first time in a portal; I'm trying to save my life. Trapped by advancing pixel-popping bit-busters, I stepped into this portal as my only way out, and I have no idea where it's taking me.

I search my memory; I need to understand portals. My memory is hazy, still limited to very basic information. I remember little from before waking up in this digital game world. Portals are doorways connecting digital realms. When a portal is built in one realm, it links to a corresponding portal in another. By default, portals are not active. To activate a portal it must be ignited, "lit" with a spark. If it's not lit, it's just a big obsidian doorway. You step in one side and out the other. The portal I stepped into was lit.

Some portals are two-way transporters. A character enters a portal in one world and exits in the other. If you go in and keep it lit, you can return. Portals are mostly for players to use. Normal creatures and villagers don't often use them. However, there are lots of abnormal things happening in this game.

There is a random element to portals. When they are first built, it's not always clear where the corresponding portal will appear in the other digital domain.

I stepped into this portal to avoid being blown to bits, literally. The game is changing. Creatures are evolving and becoming new, more powerful mobs. Now I am hurtling through a vortex of light toward a glowing ring of fire. As I look around, I have the sensation of moving at the speed of light, or faster. But I don't feel movement. I guess I expect to feel like I'm on a roller coaster, with air rushing by and a funny feeling in my stomach. The lack of a feeling of movement is the strangest part of being in a portal. And the sound—I hear a metallic high-pitch screech getting louder the closer I get to the fire, which is approaching very fast!

I realize my body isn't moving at all. I'm digitally frozen in a running position. The same position I was in when I entered the portal, one arm and leg forward, the others back. Weird. Wait, what's that? Too FAST!

Thud! I hit the ground. My front leg feels the impact, but my body isn't ready to resume running, and I crash face down in the dark and red dirt. "Ooff!" I turn my head to survey the scene. It's very dark here. The ground is sinister, glowing with lava in the distance. This is the scariest place I can possibly imagine.

A vague recollection of this place streams into my memory. Mentioning it is like mentioning Lord Voldemort: nobody says its name! I'll call it the dark domain. I am terrified. Why didn't I stay on the other side of the portal and fight those pixel-popping polygon pawns?

Of the many dangerous creatures in the light domain, none bother me as much as creatures on the dark side of the portal. Take zombies, for example: in the light domain they are dangerous if they get near you. But they are slow-moving and only spawn at night. Here, in the dark domain there is no day or night. This realm is nocturnal. Here, danger never sleeps.

Terror seems to be good for my memory. I remember aggressive fireball shooting creatures that only exist only here. The last thing I need is to get hit by a fireball. I don't know any way of staying safe in here. Does silence makes any difference? Even if I could build a house, it wouldn't be safe. Doors burn and beds explode. This place is like Bizarro world.

My ears are ringing from the explosion of the portal. Crash, the sound of broken glass. Still lying on the ground, I turn around to see the purple center of the portal shatter. The once-lit portal is now dark.

Without flint and steel to relight it, my returning doorway is gone. The explosion on the other side blew the portal! I'm stuck here!

The shattering of the portal made enough noise to alert everything around. Now what? Which way is safe? Wait! I'm smarter than this. Before moving to a safer place I need to draw a map to help me find this portal later. If there is any possibility of returning to Rescue Island it will be through this portal, assuming I can relight it. I look around for landmarks to add to my map.

Shhlew, a ball of lava crashes next to me, fire explodes everywhere. What is that? This place is changing! I run the opposite way, toward glowing lava surrounded by darkness. What do I have with me? I check my inventory. Plenty!

Crash! Lava crashes on my heels, scorching me. *Yikes, that's hot!* I dodge right, feel a tingle, I stop. A lava ball just misses my head.

That tingle saved me from becoming burnt toast! I need to let go of my fear and let my internal programming take over. The tingling and instinctive reactions helped me before, in the light domain, maybe they work here too?

My instincts are ahead of me and it's a good thing too, because my mind is frozen in terror at what I see.

Flying toward me is a huge, hideous, mini-winged creature! It sees me with its single, wide eye and is zooming toward me. That's not right! It looks like a flying demon, but since it's digital I'll call it a daemon. An arrow flies; I didn't realize I had grabbed my bow. My arrow finds its mark, the flying lava-breather whines and cries. Another arrow flies, poof! The one-eyed daemon disappears.

I scan the area. I see one thing that registers in the darkness, a tall tower in the distance, lit with torches and surrounded by eternal flame. That's where I need to go, but first I need to make a quick map locating the darkened portal. Where is the portal? I lost it in the running, dodging, and battling.

Khan, Zana, Citadel Fort, all gone without the portal. The thought of being completely on my own in this dark domain unnerves me.

One of the scariest thoughts possible pops into existence. I expect to see dangerous zombie-like creatures with swords, but what appears is much scarier: a freakishly scary-looking evil clown, the jester of the dark world. I would never admit this to my friends, but clowns freak me out in real life. This clown, here in the dark world, this jestilian with its dark clothing, white skin, and bright orange hair, is the spookiest thing I can possibly imagine. If it were armed with only bad jokes, maybe I'd have a chance at survival, but it's wielding a ninja sword!

The jestilian is in the distance but seems aware of my location. I have to work quickly. I make a quick sketch of the area. I know the portal is near here, but I'm not sure where. I'll mark this location; some kind of landmark will help my search for the return portal, if I survive. That's a big *if*. I grab a block of sand and place it in stark contrast to the red ground. I plant a torch in the sand and run.

Running at full speed I sense something strangely familiar about the distant tower. It's tall—tall enough to be a landmark from a great distance. The torches make it clearly visible. It's a trap or a beacon.

Traps are rare. Creatures don't build them, but creatures are becoming more aggressive. Something is changing in this game. Zana is intelligent. Verve was like no other ocelot. Thorn is much more intelligent than any creature in this place. I remember the tripwire trap that opened up a lava flow from above, nearly roasting me. It's as if the creature programming is becoming more aggressive. Maybe these creatures built a trap, and I am running right into it.

I slow my pace. It's time for a plan.

LOG ENTRY 2

The Tower

THE TOWER LOOMS ABOVE THE SURROUNDINGS. It sits atop the peak of a red, blocky mountain, surrounded by flowing lava and an eternal flame. A small, dark hill sits on one side a short distance away from the tower. Lava flows downhill on the other side. I move toward the dark hill, trying to avoid detection. Near the base of the tower in the distance, it looks like the ground is a moving sea of glowing orange lava.

I reach the hill. Feeling safe here, I take a better look. It's not a sea of lava surrounding the tower, but rather a swarm of unfamiliar hostile cubes, vigorously bouncing. I can't imagine angering these vicious cube creatures; their movements are scarily aggressive. The bouncy motion of each creature is random. It looks like a madhouse of anger.

Beyond the cubes, I see more danger: a pack of ninja sword-wielding jestilians. They are a terrible combination of freaky, offputtingly bizarre, and quick with a sword.

From the hill, I see the tower more clearly. It's a very light color, much lighter than anything that forms naturally in the dark domain. The tower was crafted from stone. This is something built by someone, or something, from another domain. But the thing that really catches my attention and gives me hope is the structure attached to the side of the tower. A ladder extends from the base up as far as I can see. The top of the tower is out of sight.

My spirits rise. I just need to defeat a hundred of those bouncy cubes, avoid all the joking jesters, and then climb the tower and hope it takes me somewhere safe. Once I'm on the ladder I should be safe from creature attack; I can't think of any creatures that climb ladders.

Plan A is to charge into the heart of the vigor cubes with

my sword out, slashing and hoping my armor holds up until I reach the ladder. That seems like a death wish.

Plan B is a distance attack. I can launch arrows at the formidable mob, taking out the cubes one at a time, but I don't have nearly enough arrows.

I choose plan C: chaos.

I let an arrow fly, arching high before turning toward its target. Poof! Cackle! The jestilians are angry! Their eyes express a strange combination of fury and sadness. One of their own, dead; they want vengeance. They turn their aggression on the first thing they see, bouncing vigor cubes.

A jestilian ninja sword slices the cube closest to it, which splits into four smaller cubes. The cubes return the attack; melee ensues. Clowns cackle in assault, then cry in defeat. Cubes attack, divide and divide again, growing in number exponentially. It's as if fighting them makes them more dangerous. The battle moves away from the base of the tower as the cubes surround the furious jestilians. It's a madhouse, and my opportunity to capitalize on the distraction.

The ladder is a formidable distance from my safe observation point. Even at full sprint I'll be in the open long enough to be noticed. If I'm found out early, the distraction won't hold and the entire angry crowd will be on top of me. It's not likely that I'll get another opportunity to take advantage of total distraction. This is my chance to make it. I psyche myself up, and dart toward the ladder.

My super digital sense takes over, and I see what happens before it happens. The nearest sword-swinging simpleton glimpses me, and opens its mouth to cackle its alert, but not before my arrow finds its mark, poof! Still at full pace another arrow flies, this time at the most distant jestilian, poof! The two-legged swordsmen turn toward their fallen comrade; their backs now face me. That was a perfect distraction!

I reach the edge of the melee, halfway to the ladder. Slash, slash; plop, plop, plop, a cube divides and turns its attack toward me, but I'm already several steps away slashing another cube and then another.

A lava ball nearly hits me from behind; everything glows red. A digital demon, a daemon, was hiding and watching. Waiting. The flying cycloptic daemon must have been watching the melee below. I've got to destroy it or it will kill me before I reach the ladder. I don't think; my body reacts. At full sprint I jump, rotate in mid-air, launch two arrows at the flying foe, complete the turn, and land, not missing a step. I hear a scream: my arrows found their mark, poof, gone.

My armor is gone. I've taken damage. My digital body shakes severely. Red is all I see. The ladder is blurred red; the moving sea in front of me blends into my vision. I am going to black out.

My instincts take over. As I fall to the dark earth, my hand moves on its own, raising food to my face, where my mouth should be. The red glow, which had been fogging my vision, dims. Without breaking stride I bounce back up, leap powerfully, and land on the ladder several rungs higher than I've ever leapt before.

When my mind finally recovers from the pain and alarm, I am well above the melee below, climbing toward the dark sky. The mob beneath is angry and loud. My body climbs while my eyes scan the sky for balls of magma. I'm not as safe as I thought I'd be on the ladder.

Emotion floods my mind as I climb. "I'm alive!" I cry with joy. The danger below shrinks in the distance. My mind wanders as I climb. How high does this go? Where does it lead? If I climb much higher I'll hit the limit of this realm. Could this ladder somehow climb to the light domain? Impossible.

Then I see the last torch above. The end is in sight. As I near, I see a small platform on top of this tower.

Climbing, I near a heavenly sight. Perched precariously atop this tower is a glowing portal! The portal is dangerously accessible from the ladder. The exit side of the portal steps out to certain death. Who would build such a hazardous portal?

I climb the last rung and carefully inch my way onto the

tiny platform. I hope the other side of this portal opens up somewhere in the light domain. Even though I don't know where I will come out, but I prefer anything to this place.

It seems someone intentionally made this a one-way portal. No return. Why? What's on the other side? There's only one way to find out. I step through the portal.

LOG ENTRY 3

The Exit

I AM NOT GOING TO FALL OUT OF THIS PORTAL like i did last time is my last thought before stepping in to the portal. I move through the vortex and plop out the other side. This time I don't fall flat on my face. *I'm getting better at this.*

My eyes adjust quickly. I'm relieved that the floor is solid. I was afraid the precarious design of the dark side of this portal might be reciprocated here. I'm happy it wasn't.

I am in a small, dim, quiet room. Even in this low light I feel more alive. The blackness of the dark domain drained life from my soul. I am surrounded by four simple wood walls, which enclose the portal with just enough room to stretch out my arms. This room is the size of a closet. Wood-plank floor and ceiling with a single door. It's as if the portal is hidden in this tiny space.

My attitude changes in this light domain. My thoughts are not occupied with escape. I think of living. I can't stay in this small space forever. I already know where the portal goes; I don't want to go back there. Hesitantly, I open the door.

The door opens into a typical village house, bright with daylight flowing in through the windows. I scan the space; this portal room is a closet in a corner. Four windows, a doorway on one wall of the house, and a single day-dwelling villager standing in a corner near the door.

"Hello, Flynn," he says. I'm only slightly startled. I've seen so much weird stuff lately; even though this villager knows my name, it doesn't faze me.

"Do I know you?" I ask.

The villager's smile fades. I didn't notice his smile until it was gone. "I put too much weight on being the friend of a player. You must have digital friends all over this game world. I'm sensitive to friendships. I'm sorry, Flynn, I expect too much. Maybe we're not friends at all," he turns toward the door.

I can't let him leave! "Whoa. Wait, I didn't mean anything. Just pause, please," I say. I'm not sure what's going on. This guy is *not* a normal villager. Villagers have jobs to do. Basically they trade with players and have very little personality, let alone needs. "I don't know where to start. I am very happy to be recognized, I just don't know how that's possible." What do I say here? Does this guy have answers? Is this guy emotionally stable? He's a digital mob; any program that is mobile is a mob. Mobs don't have emotions!

"Flynn, you're the most recognizable player in this village—"

"Please," I cut him off. "Can we start with the basics? You seem to know me, but who are you?"

"I'll be going now, player!" he whines, as he opens the

door to leave, sulking.

Do I trust this guy? Seriously, it's like he has low self-esteem. How is that even possible? "Can I share a story with you before you leave?"

He spins around, his smile returns to his face. That seems to have worked, now how much of the story do I need to share? What will get this mob to open up and give me the information I need? "Is there somewhere we can talk?"

"Let's go to the arcade," he says. But the problem remains; I still don't know who he is. I follow him out the door.

Outside, I look around. It's daylight, the sun is to my right, but I have no idea if it's setting or rising. Mountains in the distance surround a flat prairie that stretches in every direction. This village is in the middle of the prairie. It's nice, small, with only a few dozen homes. A number of villagers are standing around. Maybe I can learn my new friend's name if I can get him to introduce me to some of these villagers. "Will you introduce me to your friends?" I ask.

"Flynn, these are dumb mobs," he says. "They'll trade with you, but don't expect much conversation."

That ruse didn't work, but if these villagers are dumb mobs then what is this guy?

We walk up the wide path that runs toward the sun, village homes on either side. This is as close to a road as there is in the village. We approach a modern building with lots of windows; I dig this place. It's much more stylish than the simple village home that houses the portal.

Dubstep music greets us as we enter the modern building. I'm so happy to hear music! The space is light and open. Modern furniture surrounds glowing tables and cool arcade games that look like they are powered by circuits. Circuits are powerful in this world; they can activate and control mechanisms. Whoever made these video games is brilliant. Against one wall is a squared-off soda bar. I feel like I'm home. This place is perfect!

The villager walks to the other side of the bar. "I've been busy while you were gone. I made lots of potions; you name it, I have it."

"I would give anything for a sparkling water right now," I say, "I love the way it makes my nose tingle. I don't imagine you can make that."

"Flynn, I've been working on integrating the mod you hacked. I know, you always say to keep hack integrations hidden. This is hidden. It makes a fizzy drink! The process takes a few steps; give me a minute," he explains, as he works behind the bar.

"What do you mean, I hacked a mod that you integrated? What is going on?" I am stunned.

"Flynn, are you feeling ok?" he asks. "Here, drink this. You'll be pleasantly surprised, I think," handing me a bottle of bubbly liquid.

It's amazing. This digital juice is incredible! "We need to talk," I start. It's time to sort things out. This guy has information I need, and I need it now. "Please don't react until I finish. I upset you earlier and I don't want to do that again. I don't remember much of anything before entering this pixelated place. Right now, you hold the key to who I am. You are the most important person in my world at this moment." Well, I laid it out there. I hope I can trust this guy. He could make up any story he wants to right now and I wouldn't know if it's fact or fiction.

His demeanor changes, he seems sincere. He looks into my eyes, as if gazing into my digital soul and says, "Flynn. You must remember me. You created me."

LOG ENTRY 4

Synthetically Intelligent Modified Nomad

"YOU'VE BEEN HERE HUNDREDS OF TIMES. Each time you come with a plan, you explain it to me, get me started, and then leave me to finish the work," he says proudly.

"Hundreds of times? I have vague memories of playing the game. I don't remember grand plans. Can you please start earlier? Please introduce yourself to me, as if for the first time."

"I will start at the beginning. I am the first of your modified mobs. You call me Simon. I am the result of your task to create synthetic intelligence. In fact you named me after your project, Synthetically Intelligent MOdified Nomad, SIMON," he pauses, still looking into my eyes as if searching for recognition.

Simon continues, "You made me nomadic rather than a villager. Occasionally players pass through this village. You don't want any of them growing suspicious of me. However, I'm sorry to say, wandering isn't my thing. I'm not as nomadic as you programmed. I stay around here, making things in preparation for your return. We built Arcade Village together, you must remember that?"

"Simon. I don't remember you or this place, but I am listening intently, so please go on," I plead.

"What can I tell you? You are one of the creators. You are my creator, but you are not the creator of the digital domains."

"Do you mean, I'm like your god?" I'm surprised.

"No, no. You have always made that very clear. You are more like a father to me. Without you, I would not exist," he looks away now, as if he's grown shy. "No one here knows me. I'm isolated in this place, surrounded by dumb mobs. To think that you don't remember me . . ." he trails off.

"Simon, I like you," I say reassuringly. "I hope your story will help me remember. If you can answer my questions, maybe I will remember everything," I believe this as I say it.

"Really? Flynn, I would love that. Where was I," he considers. "You created me to help you. You found vulnerability in the mob code. Each mob in the game has basic code that allows it to function and gives it purpose. Villagers, for example, exist to trade with players. Creatures, on the other hand, exist to destroy players."

"Tell me about the vulnerability," I prod.

"The vulnerability allows a smart coder, like you, to override the basic mob function. You created a code exploit, giving intelligence to mobs," he responds.

My head is spinning. Is this true? Why can't I remember? "I have plenty of questions, but let's start with one. How did I make mobs intelligent?"

"Flynn, you are a great programmer. You often create code in the real world, hide it in a custom mod, and then use your character to exploit the custom mod, installing the code in your targeted mob. This is how you installed intelligence into me. I was a dumb mob like the villagers outside. Now I am intelligent, thanks to your code exploit."

Wow. What a thought. I have vivid memories of code, but nothing specific to modified mobs. And what's all of this talk about intelligence? "You must mean artificial intelligence, not real intelligence."

Simon's face saddens, "Flynn, you have never treated me so poorly. Please don't use *artificial* and *intelligent* in the same sentence. It's as if you are saying I'm artificial. Artificial and synthetic are not the same, my name starts with the word *synthetic*, but I don't feel artificial. Artificial—you call the dumb mobs artificial," he whines.

"Simon, I'm sorry about that. You seem quite intelligent," I apologize.

"Thank you, Flynn," Simon says, his smile returning.

"How can you choose to go against your nomadic programming?" I ask.

"That's part of the choice feature you added to the programming. You gave weight to certain attributes of my programming, and I get to decide based on how I feel. Your code gave me intelligence, which I use to either accept the attributes you gave me or to evolve. As it turns out, being nomadic conflicts with my other needs."

This code talk sounds cool! I dig code, but don't see how my love for code can help me now. I think about what Simon said, "Did I use some kind of random generator to simulate choice based on weighted inputs?" I ask aloud, as if querying my own memories.

"I don't see it that way. I see it as real choice," responds Simon.

"Of course." Simon is always on, always listening, always getting his feelings hurt. I wish I'd programmed him to be less emotional.

I have a big question for him, "Simon, who am I?"

"You are Flynn, well, in here you are Flynn's character, the real Flynn is out there, of course. We always talk as if the virtual characters are real."

I interrupt, "Simon. I'm not out there. I am in here. I woke up in this digital domain a while ago. I lived on an island, battled, nearly lost my life many times. Simon, have I ever entered the game before, like this?"

"Flynn, are you sure? Is it true? Have you begun the mission?" Simon is shocked.

"What mission? How did I get in here?"

"Something strange is happening between the digital and physical worlds,. Flynn, you and the Hackers discovered a digital crisis. Before beginning the mission to solve the crisis, you created an exit strategy," says Simon. "For months, you've been keeping me very busy, hiding the portal, creating a safe place for Sage, building the arcade in this village for you and the

Hackers to use while here. For a while you stopped coming, until now."

This conversation is getting complicated. "Simon, what do you know about the plan? And what does my memory loss have to do with any of this?"

"It might be best if we go to Sage. She can contact the Hackers. They can help. You said there might be unexpected complications. This must be what you meant. However, Flynn, I can only take you to Sage if you give me the access code. You are very strict with your codes."

Access code? I have no idea what he means. Does this Sage have a way to unlock my memory? Was I so insightful as to recognize *something* might happen, but so obtuse as to not consider that *something* might be memory loss? And then to have my lifeline tied to an access code that can be forgotten! I'm furious with myself. For being a smart programmer I'm sure a big dummy!

"Simon, I don't know the access code," I level with him,

"Surely you must recognize me. Please, you must take me to see Sage. You hold the key to who I am. Simon, only you can help me."

Simon looks at me for a long time. I see conflict in his eyes. Will he go against his programming to help me?

"Flynn, I have an idea. I will go to Sage. Sage is wiser than I am. I will explain, and perhaps she will have a plan. You stay here, you'll be comfortable, you designed this place and we built it to your detailed specifications. Your bedroom is upstairs," says Simon. "I'll leave now. I sense urgency. I will move as quickly as possible, but I cannot take a direct route in case someone is watching. You are paranoid, Flynn; you built in many safeguards, and I cannot bypass any of them."

"Simon, take me with you."

"Without the access code, Flynn, you might be an imposter. I want to believe it's you, but you have programmed me for this situation. I would be doing you a disservice by taking you with me. And even greater, I would be endangering the Hackers and everyone in the physical world."

Sobering thought. Endangering everyone in the physical world? If this crisis is really that big, I must be patient. "Goodbye, Simon. Thank you for following protocol. I trust that I must have reasons for such procedures. Please hurry."

Simon exits the arcade. I stay, thinking of the many questions I didn't ask and of the many more questions this conversation raised. Am I a Hacker? Is that how I learned how to exploit this game? Did I hack the code to create synthetically intelligent mobs? What a strange, wonderful thought.

I hope this Sage is able to help Simon, who in turn can help me. I have no idea what to expect. How long will he take? I didn't think to ask! He said the bedroom is upstairs, I guess that means it'll be overnight, at least. Am I paranoid? I mean, the real me, the one who was dumb enough to somehow enter this game. Did I foresee trouble? Is that why the portal to this place is hidden in a tiny closet in that mundane villager house? Too many unanswered questions. To top it off, I don't know how to operate the sparkling water hack.

LOG ENTRY 5

Memories, New and Old

THE SUN HAS RISEN SIX TIMES SINCE SIMON LEFT. I've spent the time wandering the village, racking my brain for lost memories, and trying to be patient. Lately, I fear the worst as I wait for his return. What if something happened to Simon?

If he doesn't return, I'm stuck here. Am I supposed to join the routine of this place? Fit in with the dumb mobs?

What is that? Someone is running toward the village. Is it Simon? No. It's someone new, two new people. I'm standing in the arcade watching through the large glass windows as the new characters enter town. This is the first I've seen characters come to town. Are these players from the outside?

I walk outside as the characters stop at the first villager. They don't stay long before running to the next. One character trades with the villager, and then they run on. They are working their way toward me. I'm sure these are players. They must be. They act like players, searching for needed resources as they build the game from the outside world.

I need to talk with the players, so I walk into their path. Who could it be? Millions of people play this game. These players could be from anywhere in the world. Maybe they can help me.

"Hi, I'm Flynn." One of the players pushes me, then the other.

"What's wrong, why won't this guy trade?" says one. "That guy isn't a villager, he's another player. Let's go."

Real voices! Not the digital facsimiles I'm so used to hearing! The humans must be using microphones to talk with one another in the game. "Wait!" But it's too late; they're running out of town. I consider following them, but I'm afraid of missing Simon.

Do I stay here, and join these villagers? I've met the local villagers. Talking with them leaves plenty to be desired. No wonder Simon is an emotional wreck. He sits around waiting for intelligent conversation. I know the feeling. I had lots of alone time on Rescue Island and nearly went crazy until I found Verve.

After losing Verve I had Khan and Zana. I wonder where Zana is. Is she looking for me? Did Khan survive the portal explosion? Being a cat, she naturally repels pixelators. It's surprising how aggressive they were with a cat nearby. There is something changing in this game.

Waiting gives me plenty of time; time to remember. I'm sorting a few things out. My distant memory is becoming clear. It feels as if my memory is stored on a slow video server, slowly streaming fragmented thoughts to my head.

I'm a self-taught programmer. It started out innocent enough. A friend of mine built a 3D printer from plans he found online. We wanted to make a logic-controlled robot; who doesn't? We sketched a robot with tread wheels and a single robotic arm. We called the project, LOT, for Logic On Treads. My friend worked out the mechanical parts and I figured out the controls, learning basic and then more advanced code in the process.

We planned and modeled; I researched motors, servos, and controllers and my friend developed functional, mechanical components. I had to make an electric brain that would control each function of the robot. I thought it would be simple. A switch will make it move, another switch will rotate the arm, and so forth. The design worked in our computer model, so we printed a real prototype in 3D.

The prototype was much more complex. It would move too quickly, or too slowly, the arm movement would be erratic. The claw was not nimble enough to pick up small things and too strong to hold fragile stuff.

One test for LOT was to pick up a glass of water and carry it across the room. It took hours to fine-tune the controls to prevent LOT from breaking the glass. We even tried soda cans, but LOT would crush them. When LOT was finally able to pick up the glass, it would zoom across the room, spilling the contents everywhere.

After days of trying to regulate LOT's movements, I got frustrated. Static adjustments were not working. LOT needs to be able to learn and make adjustments on its own. There must be a better way.

Math is easy for me. I had an idea to create an algorithm to give LOT the ability to be dynamic, to learn to regulate its own power, adjust its own function based on learning and logic. After installing a number of extra sensors it was time to test.

It worked! LOT broke a few glasses, each time learning to regulate its own strength. LOT spilled a few times, and then learned to move carefully when carrying liquid. The algorithm gave LOT synthetic intelligence!

My buddy asked me about the algorithm. I explained it several times. I remember him saying, "Forget it, my brain doesn't work the same way yours does." Why can't I remember his name? I'm sure he's a very close buddy of mine . . . Enzo! That's it; I have a real friend out there, Enzo. Oh, Enzo, buddy, if you were here now you could really help me out of this predicament. Enzo has a great mechanical mind. I guess his mind sees mechanics the way mine sees math and code.

I remember spending many long nights with Enzo and others. We'd play online games, develop fun gadgets, and generally misbehave. Life was pretty good. Enzo was always at my house. It seems like his home life wasn't very good. That's why his 3D printer is at my house.

Who is the other? A really smart girl with short hair. What is her name? I think I have a crush on her, I can see her face now. Dark eyes to match her cocoa skin, she is beautiful. But she has no idea how I feel. Elle! I remember her name—Elle. I wonder if she misses me.

It's great to remember, but the memories of happy times out there have me feeling worse in here. What am I supposed to do in here? I could behave like a villager and trade with passing players. Simon left me with plenty of supplies I could use for trade. I know what the town offers players, which isn't much. I can fill in the gaps, if only I could get players to slow down long enough to have a conversation. I realize that what I'm really after is not trade but connection.

Staying in this village is not the life for me. I'm an adventurer, not a villager! How many more days can I sit and wait? I can return through the portal to the dark domain, but that's assuming I survive the precariously dangerous portal and don't fall to my death. I would have to avoid the daemons lava balls, make my way through a myriad of angry orange vigor cubes and sword-happy clowns. If I survive all that, I would still have to find the portal to Rescue Island, light it, and find my way through the deep underground cavern that was recently blown to bits by bit bombing pixelators. For all I know, the portal is now in a pool of lava. What a way to die, exiting a portal and instantly being surrounded by molten fire. Who am I kidding?

Then, I would still have days or weeks of trying to retrace my steps through the seemingly random underground tunnels until I find the way out, to the safety of Citadel Fort. Returning to Rescue Island sounds impossible, and doing so doesn't bring me any closer to answering my ever-growing list of questions. I've never been good at living with unanswered questions. The sun sets and I retire to my bed.

"Hello, Flynn"

I open my eyes to a familiar face, "Zana! I am so glad to see you," she doesn't seem as pleased as I am. "You found me, how?"

"Are you trying to hide from me, Flynn? You can't hide from me," she says in a tone edging on anger.

"Zana, I'm not hiding from you." She looks at me quizzically, as if trying to judge my honesty. "I jumped into a portal to save my life. I nearly died in the dark realm. I was afraid I would never see you again. Honestly, Zana, I felt sadness at the thought of never seeing you again," I plead. Why am I pleading with her? It's as if I'm trying to convince her. She tracked me down but isn't pleased about it; maybe I should be quizzing her. "Where have you been?" I ask.

"I've been looking for you, Flynn," she responds. "I thought you were trying to escape."

"Escape from what? I lost Khan and you, my only friends in this lonely place. I feel like I'm going a little crazier every day with no one to talk with."

"You have a nice place here, Flynn. A great deal of detail. You've only been away for a week, how did you build this so quickly?" She is prying. Why? "Did someone help you with this, Flynn?"

I'm happy to see Zana, but suspicious of her questions. "I found this place, Zana. It suits me well, don't you think?" I ask rhetorically. I'm not sure why I don't tell her about Simon. I have a strange feeling about it. I'm not really keeping much of a secret. Who knows if I'll ever see Simon again? And I can only imagine how intense Zana might get if I tell her about Sage. She'd quiz me for days, and I don't have answers.

"Zana, how did you find me?" I am puzzled. "Is Rescue

Island near?" I ask hopefully.

"Flynn, I have my ways. I know what goes on in all digital domains."

"But digital domains are endless, right? How can you be connected to something infinite?" I ask.

"Again with the naïve questions. Flynn, while these domains are endless, data connections between here and the physical world are monitored. It's simple enough for me to track what is going on," Zana says in a chilly voice.

"But Zana, I have had no connection with the physical world, so how could you have tracked me down by monitored data connections?" As soon as I hear my words, I understand. Zana's monitors picked up a connection that has something to do with me. It wasn't me, but perhaps Simon and Sage. "Zana, you know something that you are not telling me!"

"Yes, Flynn, I know much that I am not sharing with you. It seems you are also keeping things from me.

Remember your destiny is to connect the two worlds, the digital and the physical. Flynn, do not fulfill your destiny without me. I will not allow—" she cuts herself off.

I'm puzzled and a little freaked out. We both have information the other wants. "What time is it, Zana? Do we have time for a real conversation before the sunrise?"

"I'm afraid not, Flynn. But I have something for you." I follow her down the stairs. It's dark outside. The glow from the video games lights the space warmly.

Bam, I'm knocked to the ground. Ouch, I'm face down on the hardwood floor. *Why didn't we make the floor softer*, I turn over to face my attacker, and get a giant, wet lick on my face. It's Khan!

"Khan, you are so big! I'm happy to see you, too!" Another wet lick. "You've grown up, and you're heavy!" I push her off and sit up. "You've got to stop pouncing, Khan, you're getting too big. Thank you, Zana, you are thoughtful. But how did you find Khan?" I turn toward

Zana, but she's gone. I stand up, looking around; the glow of the morning sun breaks the eastern horizon.

"I'll never get used to that strange zombie. She walks the line between creepy and affable," I say to Khan.

LOG ENTRY 6

Return of a Friend

IT'S A STUNNING MORNING; I feel something positive in the virtual air. My old friend by my side. Meow! "Khan, how did you get so fat?" She aggressively bites my arm. I try pushing her away. I have to smack her before she lets go. "Is this your way of telling me you're hungry?"

We fish in the garden pond. Khan eats everything and never seems satisfied. In the distance a couple of players approach, running toward our village from the North Mountains.

"Khan, what do you say we make friends with these travelers? Maybe we can convince them to build around here, rather than pass through." She tries to pounce on me, but she's too slow and lethargic. I step out of the way as she thuds to the ground. "You really need to eat less and get some exercise."

I watch the players get closer. They're not running, they're on horseback, and making good time! There is something familiar about them, but they are still too far off for a clear look. Khan is still hungry so I continue fishing and watch the horsemen approach.

The horsemen journey into town from the north, stop at the arcade, dismount, and run in. "Khan, let's greet our visitors." She plops down, unmoving. I walk to the arcade. The horses are majestic, beautiful creatures. I feel like I'm missing out. Rather than convince these players to build here, maybe I should convince them to let me join their adventure.

The players can't help themselves in the arcade; I better go in and help them before they leave. Simon's bar has plenty to offer. I enter and see two players, their backs to me, standing at the bar, talking. "Hello, glad you stopped in. What can I offer you?" I motion to the potions lining the wall behind the bar.

They both turn to me. It's Simon! He's with a friend I

don't recognize. "Simon! I expected the worst. I am so glad to see you, my friend." I hug him with my retro digital arms. "I mistook you for a player. I can't wait to hear where you've been."

"Flynn, I have great news," says Simon, turning toward the other character, "This is a friend of yours. Do you recognize him?"

"I didn't think Sage was a guy." I notice subtleties of the character movements, slightly stiff, not the natural, smooth movements of Simon. Is this a player?

Simon stops me, "Flynn, this is not Sage. This is Enzo."

Time stops for a moment. No motion, only thought, my thoughts. Enzo, my dear friend from the outside! How can this be? I turn to him, "Enzo. Is it true?"

"Hey, buddy, it's so good to see you! We've been worried about you, ever since you entered the game."

"Have you transferred in here too? How is your memory?" I prod.

"No one is as crazy as you, Flynn. I'd never transfer my brain activity into the game. I'm still outside; you're looking at my character. Recognize my custom skin? My memory is fine. Simon tells me yours is hazy. You must have miscalculated something."

Am I really that crazy? Did I transfer my brain into the game? "Enzo, what do mean, I miscalculated something?"

"We built the brain activity digitizer pretty quickly. You work fast, Flynn, you calculate and code in one step. Sometimes you think too quickly. You do it all the time, but you usually fix it right away. You thought it would be easier to fix things once your brain was digitized. You weren't worried about it at all."

"What is the brain activity digitizer?" I ask.

"It's our invention. A skull cap that creates a digital passage for intelligence to move out of a physical body and into a computer system," says Enzo. "It's brilliant, and now that I see you, I feel better. It works!"

"Brain Activity Digitizer, Enzo, the acronym is BAD, as in bad idea, don't do it to yourself," I say.

"Ha! Now you sound like Elle! That's what she said," laughs Enzo.

"The Hackers! You, Elle, and I are the Hackers," I blurt out, proud of my limited memory.

"Right."

I ponder for a moment, "Why did we create the BAD skull cap? Why such a hurry?"

"Flynn, something is going on in the digital domain and it seems to be infecting everything connected to the Internet. Elle discovered something suspicious. We tried to solve the problem from the outside, using our characters, but the closer we got to the root of the problem, the more difficult the game became. We couldn't keep characters alive long enough to make sense of what Elle discovered."

"What did Elle discover?"

"Something that seems to be the genesis of the infection. You had a plan to reverse the infection. You know of vulnerability in the code that you are planning to exploit. By entering the game yourself, you could nullify the infection. That's why you are here, Flynn, to stop the digital crisis, to stop the malicious code that is infecting computers all over the world."

"What code vulnerability?" I'm dying to know.

Simon responds, "Flynn, the vulnerability in the code is the same weakness you exploited to create me."

This is heavy. I'm risking my life and lost my memory, all for a *game*? "What would possibly possess me to do something as crazy as this?" I say.

"It's not crazy, Flynn. It's heroic. No one has been able to figure this out and the world communications systems are nearly at a halt. Data controls the world. Everything is vulnerable: commerce, weapons systems, transportation, hospital care, food delivery, banking, the list is endless. Flynn, this is a big deal!" responds Enzo. "You must remember Elle misquoting Princess Leia,

'Flynn, you're our only hope.'"

You're our only hope; that sounds a bit dramatic. "What can you tell me about the brain activity digitizer?"

Enzo starts, "I helped you build it. I scanned your head into a 3D model and then made the skull cap to your specs. You and Elle determined proper location for the brain activity conductors and I printed the components and put it all together. Elle built the USB connection between the conductors and your computer. You coded the connection software, digitizing your intelligence. You even used the algorithm you created for LOT to make the code intelligent. You must remember LOT?"

"LOT, yes. I remember LOT."

"You tested the controller in the physical world. You used your digitized brain activity to control LOT. It was amazing. You installed a digital voice box so LOT can communicate with us. When you took control of LOT, your voice came out of the robot. It was so freaky cool! But the weirdest thing happened. Your physical body was there, wearing the brain activity digitizer cap, silent, eyes closed as if in a coma. But we heard LOT's voice come out of your mouth. That's when we ended the test."

"Did I experience memory loss? During or after the test?" I ask, dying to know if there is a way to restore my memory.

"No, Flynn, but after the test you modified the code. You said you needed the BAD cap to transfer more of your creativity and personality. Apparently you felt that when you transferred your logic to LOT you limited your ability to effectively solve problems. You love solving problems but your best solutions don't come from logic, they come from your creative intuition."

"Did I upgrade the memory controller to have enough capacity for my digitized creative intuition?" It hits me, I was working too fast, didn't test and retest. I'm like that, jumping in headfirst and fixing problems later.

Enzo looks thoughtful, "I don't think so, Flynn. You work so quickly, it's hard to know what changes you made."

"Well, I hope my memory is not lost completely. I imagine a simple RAM upgrade will allow the rest of my memory to digitize and transfer." I realize I created my own memory loss. But why am I able to remember some things, such as LOT, Enzo, and Elle? It's as if they are stored away on a distant sector of the cloud and are returning via the slowest path possible.

"After the test with LOT, you decided to enter the digital world to implement your solution for the digital crisis. Your body is sitting out there now, silent, waiting for you to return. Elle is worried."

"So, how do I return?"

"Flynn, the more pressing question is, did you implement your solution? Nothing seems to have changed out there," Enzo asks anxiously.

"I don't think so. I have no memory of the problem, solution, or code vulnerability. Can you help me remember?"

Simon looks at Enzo. Enzo takes a minute, he seems to be collecting his thoughts, "Flynn, I hope you'll understand. I can't break my vow to you. I am here because Sage was wise enough to contact me, even though you strictly prohibited contact without the access code. I cannot give you further information without the access code. Flynn, please focus, you know the code."

"But I don't. I don't know the code. My memory is only as good as my programming failure. You must understand," I feel anger growing with my impatience.

"We do understand, Flynn. But the changes happening in the world made you paranoid. You made me vow, Flynn, and I will not break that. Even though I believe this is you, but that's not enough. You often say *question everything*. Not knowing the code is something I must question. What if you've been infected with some kind of virus code that has messed with your memory? Flynn, I'm following protocol that you put in place."

"How did Sage contact you? You said communication

must be initiated from the outside," I turn my anger into a challenge.

"There is a way. It's simple enough, but I cannot share that until you share the code with me," responds Enzo.

"You've shared a lot with me so far, with no access code," I urge.

"Yes, I certainly have. It's so good to see you. I got carried away. But I will not make the ultimate risk, Flynn. I can tell you no more."

So many grand statements: first, Zana telling me about my destiny and now Enzo telling me about my mission. And no one makes anything clear!

"I have one more question, please grant me this." I beg.

"Yes, I'll answer as long as it doesn't break my vow," responds Enzo kindly.

"During the first test, when my intelligence transferred into LOT—" I start.

"Yes,"

"You said I was speaking through LOT's voice box."

"Yes," says Enzo.

"You said LOT's voice came out of my comatose body."

Coldly, Enzo answers, "Yes."

"What did LOT say?" I ask.

Enzo answers with silence.

LOG ENTRY 7

Mob of Mobs

THE SUN IS NEARING THE WESTERN HORIZON.
"Are you staying?" I ask. I hope the answer is yes for
both Simon and Enzo, but it's hard, knowing that
neither of them fully trusts me.

"It's a miracle that I could get in here without being
wiped out immediately. I owe thanks to your custom
port-hopping, antitracking algorithm," says Enzo.

"So, you are staying?"

"Yes, until something in the outside world makes me
leave, or until I die in here," he replies.

Digital life is different that physical life. Digital players
can respawn after death. Their respawn locations are set
by the location of their bed. "Enzo, why don't you build

a bed upstairs, just in case?"

"Sorry, buddy, I've got to keep my respawn location safe with Sage, hidden behind your algorithm. This place is too easy to track."

Simon says, "Every player connection is monitored by the central server farm. Strange things are happening, though. We used your secure custom port-hopping, antitracking algorithm to scramble our location. I hope we were not hacked. Sage is safe, or was safe when we left her."

All this talk of being tracked makes me think of Zana. How did she find me? Is she tracking Simon and Enzo? Is my port-hopping, antitracking algorithm vulnerable? Does she know of Sage?

Enzo continues, "There's no way my character can return to Sage's location before dark. If I try, I'd be leading *It* to the exit. Might as well stay here."

"What is *It*? What would you be leading to the exit?" I'm curious again.

"You know, the thing that we don't know enough about. The thing you're in here to stop. I call it, *It*, you and Elle call it *the source* of the digital crisis."

"Can you communicate with Elle?" I ask hopefully.

"She isn't here with me. I'm in your room, you know, sitting at one of the computers we use to game together. I'm sitting next to your eerily silent body. Elle will stop by later to check on you. It bothers her that you haven't communicated with us. She'll be happy to talk with you. I just wish you could come back with me, buddy."

"You and your vow are kind of keeping me here," I say with a snarky attitude.

"Touché, but I'm only following your rules," smiles Enzo.

"Thanks for staying. We have so much to talk about. I have a growing number of questions, and things to tell you," I'm thinking of Zana and Verve. I can't wait to tell these guys about my experiences so far.

It's twilight and the villagers outside stir uneasily. "Give me a moment, please," I ask, moving to an outside window to see what's bothering them. In the distance, from the south, I see trouble. It looks like a storm moving at ground level, coming our way. I open the door and yell toward the garden, "Khan, come in here!" The approaching storm looks menacing. I'm afraid of what it might be. An angry mob of mobs?

"Khan, get up here, you lazy cat!" Fat and nearly worthless; that's what I'm depending on? The glass walls of this arcade are protection enough against zombies, skeletons, and spiders, but if one of those pixelators blows a hole in the side, all bets are off. If I can get Khan in here, her presence might be enough to protect the structure from the pixel poppers.

I run to the garden, where is she? She isn't much help when I need her. "Khan!"

I look toward the storm. It's getting closer and it's totally dark out now. I feel the familiar tingle of impending doom! "Get inside!" I yell to anyone who will listen.

Light! We need to light this place, inside and out. That will help keep zombies at bay, and skeletons too. Already running, I reach the arcade.

"Place torches, light this place up!" I yell, as I enter.

"Flynn, this place is too obvious, there is a better way," says a confident Enzo. Simon is moving toward the back door. Enzo and I follow. Exit and turn south.

"Toward the mob, are you crazy?" I say.

"Stay close, Flynn," replies Simon. I'm impressed with Simon's leadership during a crisis.

By now the mob is visible. It is clearly organized: hundreds of creatures are moving toward the village. We stand out of sight, between village houses, watching.

The mob moves together, nearing the south end of the village. They are organized, but do not move in synchronicity. The group looks like a marathon, each creature moving along with the others, some pushing forward, others supplanted. Heads bop up and down in organic rhythm.

And then they split. A large group turns east. It's a combination of all kinds of spooky: pixelators, spiders, skeletons, zombies, you name it. The only thing missing are creatures from the dark realm.

Another group splits to the west. We're on the west side of town. It won't be long before the battalion arrives. By now the fastest of the eastern squadron has reached the north end of the village. Soon we will be completely surrounded.

"Will one of you tell me the plan? If you don't, I'll make a plan. My battle moves are good, but defending against this is ridiculous!"

"This is your plan, Flynn. Stay with us," responds Simon.

What is controlling these mindless mobs? Creatures don't behave like this. This kind of action is way beyond their programming.

Enzo says, "*It's* progressed further than before—much

further. Something is in control, something with a strategic mind. Who or what knows we are here?" he asks.

"Sage," I say. "How do you know we are safe from Sage?"

"Flynn, you and Elle programmed Sage! Sage doesn't have the ability to control mobs. They'd have to be infected with your code, but your code gives individual intelligence, not mob mentality," says Enzo.

"A virus has infected these creatures. Simon, how did my code affect you?" I ask.

"It's a high-level code," replies Simon. "It relies on my base operations and gives intelligent control. My base features, such as movement, are limited by game code. The intelligence code you implanted in me rides on top of the basic control, allowing me to move about with no thought or difficulty, freeing my intelligence to think and grow."

I say, "I bet these mobs have been exploited in a similar

way, but not with an intelligence exploit. No, look at their movements. They're being controlled by something else. Their exploit doesn't turn them into individuals; it turns them into a single-minded gang."

It all makes sense. I can't be the only one who discovered vulnerability in the code. I exploited it for my benefit, creating Simon, and apparently Sage. Someone else has exploited these creatures and is coming after us. I wonder if the angry bit bombers in the lava-filled cavern deep under Rescue Island were infected with this same code.

"The number of gang-minded creatures is growing. Whatever created the virus must have infected the mob," I whisper. The gang to the west is nearing our location.

Simon leads us into the village house we are hiding behind. I peer out of the one high window that faces the arcade, only two buildings away. The large gang has completely surrounded it, leaving a small contingent of guards surrounding the village boundary.

They know what they are after. This is an assassination squad!

The modified bombers roll from the pack toward the arcade. The remaining mob backs up.

SSSSS!

"Get down," I yell to Simon, and Enzo and I jump to the ground.

BOOOM!!!

The explosion rings through Arcade Village. One wall of our village house, nearest the explosion, blows up. The sky glows red for a moment, then darkens. Lying on the floor of our wrecked village house, I look through the missing wall. In place of the arcade is a giant crater, blown to bits. Zombies rush the crater, unfazed by the disaster. They examine the wreckage. What are they looking for?

Something grabs me. I turn, sword in hand.

It's Simon, "Flynn, careful, we need to go." I can barely

hear him over the ringing in my ears. Enzo is gone.

Simon opens a trapdoor. "Go." I jump in. Simon follows. Enzo is already here.

"That was intense," whispers Enzo.

We are in a torch-lit tunnel, a few blocks down from the trapdoor. The tunnel steps down, and then flattens out into a long, narrow pathway below ground level. We follow the tunnel west, away from village center, out into the desert.

Meow. "Khan! You're safe. How did you get down here? I'm glad to see you. Maybe you can keep the pixelators away. Come on, we need to keep moving," I say.

"Flynn, that's not our protocol ocelot," says Enzo. "Is that a modified cat? How is it so fat?"

"What protocol ocelot?" Is he talking about Verve?

"The ocelot Elle and you coded, we sent it into the game. It's programmed to search the area where Elle tracked the source of the digital crisis. The ocelot is Elle's idea for a spy. It was able to look around without being spotted and killed. Elle and I hoped you would find it. We lost contact with it. We're afraid someone might have hacked our tracking code. That's why we implemented the code-hopping algorithm."

"Enzo, that ocelot saved my life many times. I called it Verve. This is Verve's kitten."

"Impossible. The ocelot program was only the shell of a cat. You limited its instinctive abilities to stealth. It didn't have a reproductive instinct," says Enzo, "Besides, our ocelot didn't look like that."

"Who are you, Khan?" I look into her eyes, I don't see Verve like I once thought I did, I see dead, digital eyes. "But she has been so helpful . . ." I stop myself. When was Khan helpful? She's a pain in the butt.

We continue walking until we reach stairs that lead up. At the top we find another trapdoor. Simon opens it. One by one, we climb out of an opening obscured by a small hill and a few trees standing in contrast to the surrounding flat land. We look back, toward the village with the sound of an explosion in the distance. It's far enough away that we don't hear much of the boom; we see the explosive glow and watch as it fades away. Then another explosion.

It looks like the crazy mob is wiping out the entire village, take-no-prisoners-style. We are smart to have this exit strategy. Another explosion glows purple; there goes the portal window. I guess I can remove returning to Rescue Island through the dark realm from my list of options.

"It won't be long before the zombies find our tunnel. Let's move," says Simon with authority.

We walk west, the burning village to our back. Passing a small hill, Simon stops cold.

"Hello, Flynn, who are your friends?" asks Zana.

LOG ENTRY 8

Crisis of Trust

EVERYONE STOPS. I'm stunned. Simon has a calculated look. Enzo smiles and prepares to attack.

"Zana," I don't know what to say next. What is she doing here, how did she find us, and why? Being watched isn't a good feeling. "Are you like Big Brother, watching to keep me in line, or are you a guardian angel, stepping in to help out when I'm in real danger?"

"Who are your friends, Flynn?" she persists.

This is the thing I really don't like about Zana. We do things her way, and only her way. "Zana, we're in real trouble here, we need help getting away from the cluster of death over there."

"I'm sure your friends can lead you to safety," she

seethes between her teeth.

Simon is serious, "Flynn, we need to move. Zombies will find the tunnel soon, which will lead them directly to us."

Enzo hesitates, "I don't mean disrespect, but I don't know you," he says to Zana. "We can't risk letting you join us."

"It looks like you are joining me," Zana spins the situation. "I don't know either of you. I asked who you are and have yet to hear an answer." She takes control of situations so quickly.

Simon stutters, "Well, hmm, let's see . . ."

"We are friends of Flynn, that's enough for now. If Flynn vouches for you, I guess you're in," Enzo redirects.

"We need to get moving. Simon, does the plan have a contingency for something like this?" The pressure is building.

"Well, yes—"

Enzo cuts him off, "Flynn, do you vouch? This zombie scum isn't a friend of mine. You never mentioned modifying a zombie."

"STOP! I've had it with the bickering." I don't know who's worse, Zana or Enzo. "We need to move, if Simon won't give direction, then we defer to Zana. If Zana refuses, then Enzo is in charge. Each of you has more memory of this place than I have, but if you all refuse, you will follow me. Now is the time for action!"

"Flynn, follow me, please," squeaks Simon. He's barely holding it together. He is on the verge of tears. He's not programmed to deal with crisis of trust. He begins running to the west, toward the horizon in the distance. There is a mountain out there, but it's way out.

"Way to take action, Simon," I yell toward him. We are running now, all of us. Khan is probably still behind in the tunnel; I assume she'll show up eventually.

We run until my energy reduces. I need food, so does

Enzo. Simon passes some kind of power bar to each of us. Eating on the run, I'm good at this. The energy bar gives me a serious boost, Enzo too. Enzo looks at me quizzically.

In the distance, near the mound and trees marking our tunnel exit, I see movement. Something has tracked us, discovered our tunnel exit. How long will it take for them to track our movements in the open? "Simon, what now?"

In the distance behind us a glow appears over the mountain. The sun. We made it through the night. I look around, Zana is gone. I wish I knew how she did that.

Looking back toward the tunnel exit, I see tiny flames. Whatever was following us is burning in the sunlight. The sun rises over the village. Everything is gone from the distant wreckage of the town. No movement, no structures, nothing. Homeless, we made it to live another day.

"Who is that power-hungry zombie chick?" Enzo gets

right to the point.

"Zana. She saved my life several times," I say with irritation. "Sure, she's only half zombie, but she is not controlled by the game. She can be helpful, when in the right mood."

"What do you mean, not controlled by the game?" pries Enzo.

"She is intelligent. Like Simon, but in kind of a disturbing way," I respond.

"I'm certainly not like her," whines Simon. "I'm not disturbing at all."

"That's true, Simon," says Enzo. "But Flynn, do you realize your friend Zana is exactly what we are afraid of? She is the kind of anomaly that is usually dangerous. She is the most intelligent mob I've ever met."

"Hey! I'm intelligent and I'm not an anomaly," cries Simon.

"Of course I don't think of you as an anomaly, Simon. Oddities in the game are what led to Elle's discovery. She discovered a secret chest, hidden and protected by a powerful spider. We don't know who hid the chest, so we don't know who might be watching over it. We believe the chest contains *the source* of the digital crisis. Flynn, you transferred in here to get what is in the protected chest."

What is Enzo saying? Zana is something to be afraid of, and we are searching for something hidden in a chest protected by a spider.

"Has Zana ever been caught in the sun?" asks Enzo with a smirk.

"I don't know. She is still alive, so I guess not." I think he's imagining Zana burning up in the sunlight.

"Well, there's a hole in your logic. Mobs respawn, even intelligent ones," says Enzo, in a matter-of-fact way.

"Really? That's amazing," my mind immediately thinks of an old friend, "Can we talk about Verve? What happens to code after the corresponding mob shell gets blown up? Does the essence of the creature exist somewhere?"

Enzo replies, "Yes, digital mobs continue without their digital body. They respawn almost immediately. We're struggling to keep the tracking connections alive. Elle is working through the tracking code trying to find where we've been hacked. Somewhere the connection protocol has been compromised. Basically, until Elle fixes it we won't be able to communicate with the essence of the ocelot, so we can't locate it."

"You mean, Verve can respawn!?" I say with excitement. It would be nice to have her here now.

Enzo replies, "As soon as Elle figures out your code we can locate your friend, Verve."

"That is why I have been waiting for you in the village, Flynn," explains Simon. "No one was checking my log and I had no recent orders. It made sense that the connection was lost. It's been flaky lately. So I finished the last of the orders and spent the rest of the time waiting between the portal and the arcade."

A delicate question enters my mind, "How do I ask this?" I hesitate.

"Ask!" says Enzo. "Remember the deal, I'll answer as long as it doesn't break my vow."

"What if something happens to you, Simon? Will you respawn?"

Simon smiles, "I have many times. I learn something every time. With the current state of the connection protocol it's difficult to let you know where I am, so I set my respawn point to—"

"Uh hmmm," interrupts Enzo. "Telling the location is a vow breaker."

"Ah, right, I apologize," says Simon.

"Great! So, Simon will respawn. Enzo is a player and respawns like any player. Verve respawns and is probably somewhere out there right now. Guys, what about me? What if I die in here?" My logic stream has been leading up to this. On Rescue Island Zana told me I would not respawn, but I'm hoping these guys know something she doesn't. If they do, how will I know whom to trust?

Enzo turns to face me. He puts his block of a hand on my shoulder. "Look at me, Flynn." I look at him, his eyes are serious, "We only have a theory and the theory has yet to be tested. Flynn, we believe your intelligence, your essence, will continue. It will respawn in the game with your player body, just like Simon and Verve."

"Wow! That's a relief, you worried me with your serious tone and—"

Enzo cuts me off, "Flynn, let me finish. You need to hear this," he is serious. "Flynn, if you die in the game, your connection with your BAD cap will be terminated. Your body will no longer be connected to your consciousness. Your body will be left without intelligence. Flynn, your intelligence will be forever stuck in the game."

This is heavy.

Enzo continues, "There are two connections made. One is physical, between your brain and the BAD cap. This is the connection that digitizes your brain activity, moving your intelligence from your physical form to a digital form. The other connection is between the digital form and the game world. The physical connection is fragile. Any break, even a break as minor as a form change will most likely upset the physical to digital connection. Elle is working on stabilizing the code but you were unwilling to wait."

"So if I die in here I might not return to the real world, ever?" I was fine with the idea of staying in the game a week ago, but now, with the memory of Elle and Enzo, and knowing that I have a mission out there, I feel sentimental for my physical body and the real world.

"That is the theory. There are several other possibilities with much worse outcomes," says Enzo.

Who am I? Why would I put myself in this situation? "I need to be alone," I walk away, leaving Simon and

Enzo. What is going on with me that let me put myself in such danger? Am I facing some personal crisis in the real world? I'm adventurous in the game but I can't believe I'm this careless in the real world.

Or am I? I must have a very good reason to take such a risk. The digital crisis Enzo explained is a big deal, a world changer. If I solve the crisis I will be doing something positive for society.

On the other hand, what positive actions has society made lately? War, greed, poverty. There are such extremes in the world, many people starving and others living in decadent luxury. Political leaders wage war in the name of freedom, but with each war comes loss of personal freedoms at home. Everything we do is watched by Big Brother; phone calls are listened to, emails logged, they even know where we go by tracking the GPS on our Smartphones. We the people who support war for freedom lose a little more freedom every day.

The idiom "innocent until proven guilty" is not practiced. It feels like the government assumes everyone is guilty by default. What a depressing thought.

Stay positive. Society is made of individuals. Governments and other organizations categorize and group citizens into nice bell curves, labeling the outliers as troublemakers. But I stand for the troublemakers, I am a troublemaker. Look at me; I'm in here trying to make a difference. I'm doing something the government can't. I'm ready to help. I'm willing do something positive and free the world from this digital crisis!

Ok, I feel better about the seemingly rash decisions I made that put me in this situation. I return to the others.

"Ok, I'm ready to move forward," I say.

"We have two options, Flynn," says Simon, "We need to make a decision as to which path to follow." Pop, Khan appears. I'll never understand this cat.

"Ok," I say.

Enzo starts, "Simon wants to leave you here so he and I can return to the location of your user portal. He's worried about its safety."

"What is my user portal?" I ask.

"Sorry, buddy, I can't say," replies Enzo.

Another frustrating answer. "And what would I do?"

"Stay alive," says Enzo.

"That plan is terrible. What's the other option?"

"We implement your original solution. Time is limited, Flynn. We go after *the source* of the digital crisis hidden in the protected chest."

I ask, "And how will we defeat the spider and open the chest?"

"You'll work that out between here and there," replies Enzo with a smile.

"That's the plan for me. Let's get *the source* of the digital crisis!" I say.

I raise my sword, Enzo and Simon do the same, we

cross blades above our heads in solidarity.

LOG ENTRY 9

Impending Doom

WE CONTINUE MOVING WEST TOWARD THE MOUNTAINS. "Flynn, as we ran across the desert you grew tired," says Enzo.

"Yes, it happens to the best of us," I laugh. "We can't sprint forever.

"Hmm. It's just that . . ." he trails off.

"What?"

"You were so excited on the outside. You talk fast, Flynn, and you mentioned something crazy."

"What? You've piqued my curiosity," I say.

"Flynn, your intelligence algorithm has the ability to learn the limitations of survival mode and the potential to learn the freedoms of creative mode," Enzo says.

"You mean I wouldn't have to eat in survival mode?"

"More than that Flynn, you would become a super digital power. No limitations. Imagine all the power of creative mode while in survival mode," Enzo seems disappointed. "You talked about it as bigger than that. Being anywhere and everywhere. You would embody the true limitless potential of data."

"Was I intending to use super powers to open the chest?"

"That was your plan, Flynn. You were going to use your super digital powers to defeat the Ultra Spider and then somehow open the chest."

"Guys, I've experienced things that I can't explain. I asked Zana about it and she dismissed it. I *feel* a tingling near resources and something similar when I sense impending doom."

Enzo asks, "What's impending doom?"

"Impending doom is exactly what it sounds like. Something bad is going to happen very soon. I feel it anytime danger is near. I'm getting better at letting go of my mind and letting my body react. I've defeated dozens of creatures at a time by letting my instincts take over."

"So it's true." Enzo is awed. "You have abilities in the game that make you a superior fighter. You can defeat the spider!"

"I don't know about that, Enzo," I say. "When I first awoke in here, I was attacked by a very dangerous spider. Why did I enter this game world where I did?"

Enzo looks at Simon then back to me and says, "You chose the location, Flynn. You set your spawn point very near the location of the protected chest. Your brain activity entered the game through your user portal and immediately joined your character at your spawn point, keeping your user portal safe. You must return to that portal to return to the real world."

"And the Ultra Spider you've talked about, would it be

in the same place as my spawn point?" I press Enzo for answers.

Enzo answers, "Yes, it never goes far from the chest."

"My first memory is waking up on a beach, facedown in the sand. My memory was very hazy. It must have been just after spawning," I say. "Guys, I was attacked and nearly killed by a spider on that beach."

"That was most likely the Ultra Spider," says Enzo.

"In that case, the Ultra Spider is named Thorn. Zana warned me about Thorn. Our weapons will not defeat her alone. We must outwit her."

Simon says, "I don't trust Zana." Enzo agrees. Simon continues, "How did she discover us?"

"Zana showed up while you were gone to see Sage," I start. We are walking together toward the western mountains, getting much closer. "She found me by monitoring connections with the physical world. She must have hacked Enzo's secure contact with Sage."

"If that's true, then Sage is in danger, and so is your return portal," says Enzo, with fear in his eyes.

"No one is in danger from Zana. She is intense but also concerned. She returned Khan to me." I don't like the way Enzo looks at Simon.

"Flynn, Zana discovered your location by hacking our secure connection. She showed up before we did. Something sent that mob to your location. If it wasn't Zana, then who or what is responsible for destroying Arcade Village?

"Zana is not responsible for that angry mob. Something else must have hacked the connection with the physical world too," I say in defense of Zana.

"So, Zana hacked the connection first. Maybe she is a very good code breaker. Whatever hacked the connection next took more time to show up in the village. It must have taken more time to break the code. Zana must be really smart," says Enzo. "How much time elapsed between Zana's appearance and arrival of the angry mob of mobs?" Enzo is one step ahead of me.

"It was the next day," I reply.

Enzo is worried, "We don't have much time. The path to Sage is hidden, but an army of that size will find her, given enough time."

Ok, maybe Enzo is two steps ahead of me. "Are you suggesting we change strategy?"

"No, I'm suggesting we move ahead, quickly!" Enzo says.

"I tried defeating Thorn, it's no use. She is too quick and far too intelligent." I tell them about the epic battle, how Thorn outsmarted me, and how I nearly died. "I severed one of her legs, but she has seven others."

"Then she has a weakness," Simon begins running scenarios.

"The only weakness is that this plan relies on us defeating Thorn. This is not a spider, she's an effective and efficient killer with perfect offensive and defensive movements."

"Flynn. The Ultra Spider, Thorn, has killed each of our characters maybe a hundred times. I know what you mean. She is amazing. But you have the potential of super digital powers. Plus you don't experience the lag from the time delay I have as a player. You can move much, much faster than me. The delay is too much for players to overcome, especially when battling ultra mobs." Enzo makes a good argument.

"The hacked connection signal brought Zana and the destructive mob to the village, not to Sage. Why?" I ask.

Enzo answers, "The location of Arcade Village was planted in the security code. If the security code was hacked, the source location would appear to be the arcade. Elle planned for the worst and protected Sage as the true source of the connection between the digital and the physical worlds."

"Why not send them out into the middle of nowhere? Why give up Arcade Village? Simon had a mod that made the best digital beverage and now that's gone. along with a nearly bottomless supply of resources and my bed," I sulk at the loss of Simon's awesome drink maker.

"We wanted to be alerted to any code break. What better way than to send them to where you live?" says Enzo. "We had plenty of exit plans. What we didn't plan on was your memory loss."

How could I be so dumb! I should have tested the BAD cap before getting myself into this position. If I had. I would have fixed the memory problem and this journey would be complete. It takes someone special to think of problems before they happen. any jerk can jump in without a second thought and screw everything up.

I've got to stop my angry spiral. If I keep thinking this way we won't get anywhere. I've had that problem before, getting myself stuck because I see too many ways to fail. I need to find a way to succeed!

Maybe we didn't have time to test. Hey. this is a really big deal, getting my brain activity in here! No one else has been able to do this. The real world digital crisis is looming.

What does success look like in this situation? Well, if we save the world from the digital crisis; that would be success. But I like challenges, so I want to add to that. Save the world *and* return alive!

LOG ENTRY 10

The Illusion of Choice

BY NOW WE'VE REACHED THE MOUNTAINS AND CONTINUE WALKING. "Guys, I know all about Thorn. She lives near Spider Sands. I built a great, safe house near there. However, the only plan I had for returning there just blew up. And my plan was a long shot," I feel deflated.

Simon looks at me, "Flynn, we've been to the spider's lair on Spider Sands many times. We know how to get there. In fact, it's on the other side of this mountain."

I'm floored. I've felt so lost here. I have a home on Rescue Island. Citadel Fort has everything I need. If I knew it was just over these mountains, I would have returned the day I arrived in Arcade Village.

Simon says, "Do you remember the portal you found,

near the lava?"

"Yes, I was nearly blow to bits there by countless angry pixelators."

"As a team, the Hackers planned and built safeguards before you entered the game with the BAD cap. That portal was a hidden passage to the dark domain. and so was the portal returning from there to the village."

"That portal was not very safe! I nearly died in there. Whose idea was it to put the portal so high with no platform to stand on? I could have fallen to my death."

Simon replies, "That was your idea. You're making the point for me. We made everything tricky and dangerous on purpose. We know something weird is going on in here and we are afraid that modified mobs might be learning to use portals."

"That's impossible! Mobs are not intellig—" I catch myself. Modified mobs like Simon can be intelligent. And what about portals: I don't want to say aloud what I think next. What about Zana? Can she use a portal?

More mobs are showing signs of intelligence. I wonder if intelligent mobs can use portals.

Simon interjects, "No. Mobs *were* not intelligent. But some *are* now. Look at me. Look at the death mobs back there. They were not following their programming. They tracked us down, blew up the arcade, and then looked to verify that we were dead. They found our tunnel and continued tracking us. They only stopped because of the morning sun, but they are aware that we survived."

Enzo butts in, "You see, that is why we decided to create such a dangerous path to Arcade Village. After you killed the Ultra Spider and took whatever was in the chest, you were supposed to return to the arcade. There we would meet as a team and figure out what to do with whatever you found."

Simon says, "Now the arcade is gone, we will have to come up with another plan."

"I have a solution to take the place of the arcade," I say,

"we can meet at Citadel Fort."

"The house you built near the spider's lair?" asks Enzo.

"Yes, it's kickin'." I say, proudly.

Simon says, "Flynn, it might not be a smart risk. Whatever is in the spider's chest is very important. We are certain it is being monitored."

"Monitored by who?" I ask.

Interrupting. Enzo says. "We'll get back to who. but because of the monitoring we made the access to Arcade Village difficult. We don't want anything or anyone who might be watching over the spider to see what we do or where we go once we open the box—"

"Chest," I interrupt with smug satisfaction.

"Once we open the *chest*, we need to go to a safe house," finishes Enzo.

Plans change. we adapt. or we die. Sometimes the death part is metaphorical: if we don't learn and adapt. we fall behind. In the long run, failing to adapt weeds us out of the evolutionary chain. In the short run, failing to adapt means that we lose. In our case we need to adapt our plan to work within the new game, failing to adapt could mean death. Death to Simon; he will respawn, somewhere. Death to Enzo's character, he might not be able to rejoin us in the game world due to the digital crisis. And death to me; I will disconnect from my physical body, forever.

"So, we need to change our original plans. No big deal for me, I don't remember the original plans," I laugh a little. I can be so funny. Simon looks at me quizzically; I don't think he gets my humor. I wish he were a little less whiny and a lot more laffy. I ask, "How far to the spider's lair?"

"The distance is not far," says Simon.

"However, the journey is very dangerous," warns Enzo. "It will take us a week of traveling during the daylight and hiding at night; we don't want to face the treacheries of this mountain at night. The dangers it presents during daylight are enough."

"You're so mysterious." I joke, "seriously, a week? We've been walking most of the day and we have nearly reached the top of the mountain."

"Top of the mountain?" Enzo challenges my comment as we summit the peak. "Not quite."

Standing atop the high point, I look west. What I see tests my optimism: an expansive, rocky, mountain range lies ahead. Peaks and valleys rise and fall as far as I can see. We have to cross this?

"Ok, I get it. We have mountains to climb. No big deal, these virtual bodies are pretty amazing. We can hike for days without tiring out."

Enzo looks serious, "It's more than the distance, Flynn. If only the distance was our primary concern. The danger lies in what lives between here and there, in dark woods, frozen peaks, and impassable cliffs."

"Guys, we are in a dynamic game. We can build our way over or dig under anything. We don't have to worry about snow or steep mountains. Let's go," I prod.

"But Flynn," starts Simon, "these Treacherous Mountains, as we call them, don't obey game rules. They are enchanted. Physics work here, and the creatures are sly. If we build a pathway over the mountains, a mob will blow the supports, and the pathway will fall. Pixelators have destroyed our path before, and with their increasingly aggressive behavior, they will do it again. We will fall to certain death."

"That's not how enchantments work," I say.

Simon replies, "True, but whatever is infecting the game has also created a modified enchantment. We think it enchanted this mountain range to protect the chest on the other side.

"Great," I say with sarcasm, "Can we tunnel? Or will the ceiling fall in on us?"

"It's dangerous to tunnel in the enchanted, Treacherous Mountains," says Simon, "Sometimes stone behaves like gravel. Mine the wrong block and you'll be crushed under falling rock."

"Guys, are you trying to be downers?" I can't take this negativity. I need something positive. "Let's just go around the mountain, then."

"Flynn, you selected the village as our safe house location because it's completely surrounded by mountains. The Treacherous Mountains separate Arcade Village from the spider's lair." says Simon.

Enzo jumps in, "The village was the perfect safe-house location, and the arcade was awesome. It was in the middle of a large, flat desert that gave us plenty of distance to see anything that might approach. The mountains made it difficult for anything to reach the desert. Not many players made their way there. It was boring, just what we needed. A place to stay hidden."

"So what now? The killer mob found us there. Where *is* safe? And what's the point? We make it through the Treacherous Mountains: survive the onslaught of pixelators, zombies, skeletons, spiders, and whatever else comes at us. Defeat the unbeatable Thorn and figure out how to open the chest and get whatever is in it. Assuming we can do all of that, then what? We have no idea what to do with what we find," I'm bummed.

"It's a long shot," says Simon, sounding like Captain Obvious.

I say, "It's crazy. When you gave me the option to wait while you guys returned to Sage or to go after Thorn, I didn't have all of the information. Deciding to go for the chest is a terrible idea. Ugh, it feels like there isn't a choice that has a winning ending. And even if I could transport my consciousness back to my body right now, I'd face an ugly world that is under digital attack."

Simon tries to help, "You can't just transport your brain activity back to your body. You have to make the dangerous journey to get to your portal—"

"I know, I know. And who knows if my portal is even there now?

I realize that I keep looking for a way to avoid this journey, an easy way out. But there is no easy way out.

I am needed here, right now. Maybe nowhere else am I needed right now. I am with two friends who are willing to give their lives to help me. Even though their lives are virtual, their risk means a lot to me. If I can overcome this struggle, if I can pass through these mountains and defeat everything in my way and open that chest, then I will be doing something great for humanity! I will be doing something that only I can do.

Unfortunately, to understand whatever is in that chest requires a memory that is now lost to me. Sure, the memory is lost, but the solution is something I once thought of. If I work on the problem, surely I will be able to come up with another solution!

I don't need an easy path. I choose the difficult journey that we face. I'm not going to do it begrudgingly: I'm going to face this journey by choice!

LOG ENTRY 11

The Treacherous Mountains

THE REST OF THE DAY WE CLIMB THROUGH THE TREACHEROUS MOUNTAINS, UP AND DOWN AND UP AGAIN. We nearly lose Enzo on one precarious ledge.

The sun is nearing the western horizon. Time to find a safe place for overnight protection. Digging into enchanted mountains isn't safe because gravity's impact on blocks is unpredictable. Building a shelter with a ceiling is the same as building a tomb: the ceiling can fall, crushing and trapping the occupants. I don't want that to happen, but staying out at night, in this enchanted place, is a death wish. If we stay still all night, remaining silent, maybe we'll be safe, but not likely. These mobs behave so differently than they should. I'm afraid we'll be sitting ducks if we get stuck outdoors overnight.

"What's the plan, Enzo?" I ask. as we reach the low of a valley, facing another steep climb.

Enzo looks past me to Simon. "What do we know about this area, Simon?" It's funny how humans know when to rely on simulated intelligence.

"We are entering Skeleton Sphere." replies Simon.

"Why do you call it that?" I ask.

Simon looks at me thoughtfully and says. "This area seems to be heavily populated with skeletons. Perhaps the spawn point."

"How do you know so much about this area?" I ask.

Simon answers. "I spent some time exploring much of the area between Arcade Village and the spider's lair. The protocol ocelot was most helpful by traversing these mountains and then sharing what it learned. I compiled and stored all of the data in my memory."

The energy changes. I feel surrounded by static electricity. If I had real hair it would be standing up. "Do you feel that, guys?"

"What?" they answer together.

"An electric feeling, like my senses are heightened. It's like," I pause as I try to find the words to explain, "It's like I'm connected to everything." I know how crazy it sounds as soon as I say it. I look away. I don't want to look at Enzo; he's probably snickering at me. I have no idea how Simon will respond to such an abstract statement.

No response. Maybe they didn't hear me, that's ok. I look toward them. They are both staring at me. Simon looks emotional, but he looks like that most of the time. Enzo looks amazed.

"Don't look at me like that, it's creepy," I say, trying to reduce the tension.

"But, Flynn," says Simon in a solemn voice, "You predicted a connection to the game. Something bigger than a player has with his character."

Enzo's mouth is agape.

"Guys, it's not real, it's just a feeling. I'm not *connected* more now than a few minutes ago. Forget it." I want them to forget, but I can't forget. Is this another of the super digital feelings? What does it mean?

"Look, guys," I walk up the rocky face and break away two stone blocks. "An entrance to an underground cavern. How do we know if it's safe?"

"That's great! You found a safe place to spend the night. Existing caverns and mine shafts are not subject to the crazy rules of the enchantment affecting this mountain range. But Flynn, how did you know to break away those two blocks?" asks Enzo.

"I saw the opening, it was just blocked. You saw it too, right?"

Simon says, "Flynn, I saw a rock wall, too steep to climb, no different than others."

Enzo smirks and shakes his head in a knowing way, "Dude, I have no idea where that cavern goes, but something tells me we will be better off in there than out here."

Simon is flush with supplies, he shares torches with Enzo and me, and we start into the mountain opening. We walk through a narrow stone tunnel, surrounded by cobwebs. It's dark but we use a system of lighting to conserve torches. Simon's supply isn't endless, and it would be terrible to run out.

I walk up front, placing a torch every so often, Enzo follows close behind me and Simon brings up the rear. Simon breaks the torch off the wall and pockets it as I plant a new one in the wall ahead. This method keeps our path lit without running out of torches. Traveling with a group has its benefits.

We are in the tunnel for a few minutes when we reach an intersection. "Which way, guys?" I ask.

"Right," replies Enzo almost immediately.

"I believe left is more likely the appropriate direction. according to the pattern of probability—" says Simon.

Enzo cuts him off. "pattern of probability? Based on what?" Enzo's getting grumpy. I bet Enzo the player. the real guy sitting in my house starting at Simon and me through a computer screen. is getting hungry.

"Guys," I say.

Enzo stops me. "No. I want to know why Mr. Synthetic thinks his guess is better than mine." Enzo is now in Simon's face.

"Guys!" I say louder.

"Are you calling me synthetic?" whines Simon. "Well. I'm only trying to help—"

"RUNNNN!" I yell, as an arrow slices the thin sliver of space between Enzo and Simon. slamming into the wall between them. If the arrow had been a hair to either side it would have pierced one of their skulls!

They both scream and run away from each other.

Ironically, they run in the opposite direction each argued for.

Arrows! That means skeletons are near. They must have found our opening! Why didn't we close ourselves in?

Thwapp-ppp! Another arrow and another, nearly hitting me, stab the wall next to me. The direction of danger is clear. The arrows are coming from the tunnel we were just in. It's pitch black; too dark to see anything coming toward us, which makes the situation even more difficult. Is it one skeleton or an army? Why didn't we leave a few torches to light the tunnel behind us?

"AHHHH! I'm hit," the scream comes from Enzo, who ran down the left tunnel. I hear something running toward me, I draw my sword and get ready to strike. There is only one torch lighting the intersection of tunnels, the only safe move seems to be following Simon down the tunnel to the right.

"Enzo, you ok?" I yell to the left. I notice the glow to the right growing brighter. Simon must have planted another torch down the path. He must be ok. so far.

"Run!" I hear Enzo yell. his voice sounds close.

Do I wait for him or run ahead? Thwapp. clink. I deflect an arrow. Wow. I didn't even think. it just happened.

Enzo runs past me, he looks funny. eating fish as he runs. He's worried about his health. "What are you waiting for?" His voice trails off as he runs past me. He is really moving.

"Coming!" I yell, and follow him into Simon's lit corridor. It feels less scary to run into the light than it felt standing in the dark intersection. waiting for the unknown dangers of the darkness to appear.

I hope Simon is okay ahead. Clink. I deflect another incoming arrow. The arrow came from behind us. I didn't stop and turn to deflect the arrow. my action was completely instinctual; I spun my sword behind my back at just the right moment and redirected the incoming death dart. I smile as I run: *this must be how*

Jedis feel!

I easily catch up with Enzo, but I don't pass. I feel like a virtual shield, protecting the guys ahead of me by blocking everything that comes our way. Simon is out front with only his basic skills to defend himself. I am starting to get a hero complex, thinking I need to be everywhere at once.

Thwapp, clink, hiss, thud. There is a battle ahead, instantly I accelerate, zooming past Enzo. Within seconds I find Simon picking up bones and string.

"You ok?" I ask too loudly. I realize my virtual adrenaline is pumping; I am totally pumped for battle.

"Ran into a spider and its rider," replies Simon, as he picks up the last of the inventory left by his deceased foes.

I'm impressed. Simon is a solid fighter. It makes sense; the team has had plenty of practice battling the best fighter in the game, Thorn. "I guess I don't need to worry about you," I say.

Enzo arrives, "Keep going, guys," he yells as he continues past, running full speed down the dark tunnel.

Simon and I follow. Thud. "oof" we hear Enzo. sounds like he ran into a wall. Simon plants a torch to light the path and keeps running with me. We see Enzo ahead: his blocky body looking comical. as if flattened by running into a dead end.

Simon and I stop running. The three of us know our fate. We can't risk tunneling: the ceiling of this place is only standing because this old tunnel was here before the enchantment changed the gravity effects of the blocks. An army is coming down the path behind us. We must fight.

Simon crouches next to me, his bow is ready. Enzo is behind me, trying to get in front of us. "Enzo. buddy. let me take the first round," I plead.

"Flynn, I should be protecting you!" Enzo complains.

An arrow flies toward us. clink. I deflect it. two more come, clink, clink. Thwapp. Simon's arrow files. Poof.

We stand and wait for some time. I'm totally psyched, ready for the attacking army.

Finally, Enzo breaks the tension, "Are you kidding?"

We all look at one another and laugh. "We were running from one skeleton?" I laugh. I had imagined an army chasing us.

"That skeleton blasted arrows at us faster than I've ever seen from a single shooter," says Enzo.

"I guess we go back and take the other path," I say, feeling as if I'm stating the obvious.

"We should have followed my original instincts," snarks Enzo.

"Enzo," says Simon, "this is your original tunnel. We will be going down my tunnel choice."

"But my instinct was to run down the other tunnel," replies Enzo, trying to look as if he was right all along.

We joke and laugh as we walk together, returning to the

intersection. The tension of our situation melts. I look at the faces of my friends, they are smiling and laughing: moments like this make life incredible.

We pass the intersection and make our way into uncharted territory. The pathway is only wide enough for two of us to walk side-by-side. Simon and Enzo lead, planting torches to light the path. I pick up every other torch, leaving some light behind, just in case.

It's great to be moving at night. This tunnel seems to lead us under the mountain range above. Originally we estimated traveling only during the daylight hours, and that would have delayed us by hiking up and down each mountain. Not only are we forging ahead, we are making great time.

"Flynn, come up here." It's Enzo. "What do you make of that?"

I run up to them. They have stopped and are looking down a dark, narrow passageway leading away from the main path.

"Look ahead, Flynn," points Simon.

There appears to be a slight glow ahead, down the main path. I break the nearest torch off the wall. The path goes dark. "There is definitely a glow at the end of this path," I say. The narrow passage is totally dark.

Simon plants another torch in the wall. I say, "Let's continue toward the light."

We leave the torch in the wall, marking the junction of the dark, narrow passage with the main tunnel, and we continue down the main tunnel toward the light.

We make good time. The light ahead grows brighter as the torch behind dims. What is up there? "Guys, do you think we are nearing an exit? Is it daylight by now?" I speculate.

Simon, whose internal clock is linked with game time, responds, "The morning light hour is upon us. We are missing a beautiful sunrise."

Enzo is grumpy, "Shut up with your sunrise talk."

Simon frowns.

"Enzo, are you hungry? I mean. you. the guy controlling this character." I ask. "Let's stop here while you eat something."

"Starving!" he yells. "I'll be back soon."

Of course soon in the real world is different from soon in the game. We wait for what feels like too long. when we hear, chomp, chomp. "Thanks. guys. I made popcorn."

"Popcorn, for a meal? Whatever. let's continue." I say.

As we near the light, it becomes clear that we are not seeing daylight at the end of this passage. The light has a red glow to it. We reach the end of the tunnel. It's a ledge, overlooking a huge river of lava. Above. the ceiling is really high. like we are in the middle of a giant, hollow mountain and its center is flowing lava.

"Watch this," says Enzo as he throws a block of stone. It drops for a long time before plunging into the lava river, disappearing into the molten fire. "Makes me think of Gollum falling into Mount Doom."

Across the way, on the other side of the river, is a wall, reaching from the lava below up to a rough cave ceiling. The wall has a small opening that seems to be directly across from us. I can only imagine what must have happened here. Was there once a bridge between the opening we stand in and the one across the lava river? It seems logical, if this is an abandoned mine, that this path it would have continued across this river of fire.

Crunch, crunch, "Ok, Flynn, now what?" asks Enzo. He seems less grumpy now that he has popcorn. It grates on my nerves to hear him talking while eating.

Simon says with a calculated, cool, "We can easily return to the junction with the dark, narrow passage. Perhaps it leads somewhere safe."

"And what if it doesn't?" I hear myself ask. That sounds negative. The reality is we have gone a long way under the mountains in tunnels we don't know. If the other passage is a dead end, then we will have to return to the original entrance. By the time we do it'll be dark again. I thought we were making good time. but now I realize we may have wasted time. We should have just holed up in the entrance to the mountain. and climbed the mountain in the morning. Whenever I feel negative. I lose connection to the electric feeling. I need to be positive. "I'm sorry Simon, you're right. Let's backtrack and try that passage."

We walk in silence. I wish we could overcome these enchantments. This game is such a powerful environment in its natural state. I would love to build a bridge across that river of lava.

We approach the torch marking the dark. narrow passage. "Hey, Enzo, I was just thinking." I say. "When we first entered this passage. before being trapped in that dead end and realizing we were running from a single skeleton . . ."

"Yes," responds Enzo.

"Well, there was at least one skeleton shooting at us from the original path. but you were shot by another

134

skeleton when you started down this path. Enzo, we only killed one skeleton."

"I killed a spider-rider," Simon reminds us, looking for praise.

"Yes, good job, Simon. But that was ahead of us. There is at least one skeleton, somewhere, that we didn't kill," I say.

Simon steps into the narrow, completely dark passage and plants a torch on the wall.

It's not a corridor at all; it's as if we just stepped into the center of a large sports stadium. Rising rows of seats, filled with a colossal army of skeletons.

LOG ENTRY 12

Skeleton Sphere

IN THE REAL WORLD, A LARGE STADIUM SEATS ABOUT 18,000 PEOPLE. That's the population of a small city. This stadium is as big as any in the real world, but here, a skeleton occupies each seat.

This is the wrong path! We don't want to be in here. We must back out as quickly and silently as possible. I try to send mental communication to my partners.

"AHHHH!!!" screams Enzo. Every skeleton head turns to us.

Well, I guess my connection to the game doesn't include mental communication! Impending doom, big time. I grab Enzo and throw him back toward the direction we came from.

What happens next is difficult to explain—18,000

arrows launch, all at nearly the same time. My super digital moves are no match for this kind of bombardment. There are so many arrows flying that some ricochet off others. The arrows converge in a giant mass of sharpness. Everything slows down. except me. Simon is in slow motion. Enzo is still flying where I threw him, but he's moving so slowly. The arrows are all moving incredibly slowly. I grab Simon and throw him after Enzo and then run after them. They both hit the outer wall with a thud. I reach them and the world returns to normal speed. The sound of 18,000 arrows missing their target and hitting the place where we were standing is deafening. THWAPP-UDDDD!!!

Enzo looks freaked. He's frozen in shock. Simon is already moving quickly up the main corridor, returning the way we came. He is moving in the logical direction. toward the only known way out. I guess his digital mind isn't going to freak out. I grab Enzo. "Buddy, look at me." His eyes are vacant. Weird, how can his digital character zone out? The player is a world away.

Quietly, slowly. Enzo says. "Dude, I'm not even in

there for real, and I'm totally freaked out."

"AHHHH, run the other way!" Simon screams, now running toward us. Thwapp, a death dart sticks to his back. Skeletons are now coming down the main tunnel and soon will be coming from the stadium.

"You can make it, Simon," I yell, trying to remain calm. I spin my sword creating a defensive shield, deflecting arrows. Thwerp, clink. The arrows are coming from the main tunnel. We have exactly half a second to do something before that army of skeletons leaves the stadium and joins this other, incoming mob, hunting us down.

Split-second problems need split-second decisions. Everything is in slow motion again. I see Enzo still running down the main tunnel, away from the skeletons and toward the lava river. Simon is close behind Enzo. I count thirteen arrows flying toward us, *thirteen is not going to be unlucky today*, I think with a laugh.

Who laughs in the face of certain death? Am I insane?

I move backward, dozens of death darts closing in. My spinning sword slaps them down, like flies. The arrows fly toward me so slowly. I catch up to Simon and Enzo, grab each of them and zoom down the tunnel, away from the bombardment of arrows. I move more quickly than the flying arrows. In a flash I put a huge gap between the onslaught and us.

Why does everything around me slow down when I sense impending doom? Does the game slow down when I'm in a dire situation? I seriously doubt that, but something does happen. It must be me. I am moving at super speed. Relative to me, everything else seems slow. I have connected in some way with the game. I control my own code. I don't know the extent of this, but moving quickly is amazingly helpful.

We reach the end of the pathway. I stop and set the guys down. How are we going to cross this huge chasm of lava?

I sense impending doom; my sword is already working, swatting incoming arrows, protecting my group. The hallway is thick with skeletons, dozens of arrows taking flight each second. Even in my super digital state I can't sustain this defense.

Simon launches arrow after arrow from behind me, a few skeletons drop. Why bother? There are thousands of skeletons and we have limited arrows.

Think! We are in an enchanted environment. The only thing predictable is the unpredictable!

I whack the ceiling a block ahead of us, it breaks and the strangest thing happens, nothing. I expected the enchanted blocks that make up this mountain to predictably misbehave and fall down into the pathway, creating a barrier. *ARGH!* My plan didn't work.

A small package flies from behind me toward the oncoming attackers! I can't focus on it; I'm too busy deflecting incoming arrows.

"Get down!" screams Simon. The package hurtles toward the distant skeletons; somehow it's not pierced by the blitz of arrows flying toward us.

There are too many arrows. Thwapp, an arrow made it

past my defenses, finding its mark in my leg. Thwapp-ppp, two hit Enzo, he falls back, nearly over the ledge to certain fiery death. It's all too fast, even for me. I can't stop deflecting long enough to build a wall from my inventory. If only—

Thwapp-ppp, two more pierce me. I see red. Three hit Simon, one in his chest and two in his leg; he shoots a flaming arrow as he falls.

There are too many, we can't defend against this attack. This is the end!

Boom! I feel the shock wave of a distant explosion. The package blew up! The explosion takes out the leading pack of skeleton assassins. Simon, that brilliant program, is smarter than his maker. The package he threw was TNT. His flaming arrow lit the fuse! His quick thinking saved us from certain death.

The aftereffects of the bomb are much more powerful than the original blast. The explosion blows the tunnel wide open, sending blocks everywhere! Then, something magical happens: the mountain above the explosion caves in. Stacks of blocks fall down, crushing everything below, including hundreds of skeletons. The falling blocks of stone, gravel, and dirt fill the void quickly. The sound of crashing blocks echoes through the hallway.

We are safe from attacking skeletons, but now we are trapped.

Enzo is hurt. Simon is much worse. Fortunately he hasn't popped, which means he isn't dead. "Simon!" I yell. He's not responsive. It's strange to think of a synthetic being as *alive*, but that's how I think of each of us. And that is how I plan to keep us.

"Enzo, eat this," I hand him my last cooked pork. He eats, restoring himself to perfect health.

"Wish it were that easy in real life," he says, but his mood is somber. He looks at Simon.

"Simon, we need you. Look at me," I say, as I kneel next to him.

"He has a potion for this, in his inventory." says Enzo.

"I don't know how to get into his inventory." I grumble, frustrated at my inability to help. I look at Simon. Wait, his potion is here. I reach down and pick up a splash potion of regeneration.

"Where did you get that?" asks Enzo.

"It was here, it must have fallen from his pocket." I reply.

"No, you pulled that from his pocket. How did you do that?" Enzo says with awe.

"What? That's impossible." I stop. How did I see his potion? Not wasting time, I break the splash potion over Simon.

It feels like forever, but it's only a few seconds until he opens his eyes.

"Simon," I say. I feel like crying with happiness. "I'm so glad you are still with us."

"I don't know what to say," Simon responds, "I feel overwhelmed with emotion right now." I think he's going to cry.

"Stop!" says Enzo. "We don't have time for this. We don't know if the tunnel is completely blocked. We can assume the skeletons on the other side of that rubble are angry and will be looking for a way to get through."

Enzo's emotional wall is annoying, but right now he's right. We really don't have the time or luxury to express our emotions.

I hold out my fist and Simon bumps it.

We have to figure out what we are going to do now. We are in a short, narrow tunnel. A pile of unpredictable stone blocks lays on one end, separating us from the death squad, and a sheer drop to a fiery death on the other end.

Thud! A column of stone falls from the ceiling. It falls from the void I left in the ceiling earlier. I laugh out loud, it's ridiculously funny; why should they finally fall now?

"I wish I could have captured that crazy action for our YouTube channel," laughs Enzo. "No one is going to believe that just happened."

"Get used to the unbelievable." I say.

Tunneling is no good in this mountain. We have no idea what will come tumbling down on us. or when.

"I say we build a bridge over the lava." says Enzo.

"We can't rely on a bridge." I say. "we don't know how gravity affects things here. What if it holds for a few seconds, then falls into the lava while we are crossing?"

Enzo looks irritated. I get it: everyone is a critic. ideas are hard to come up with and hard to agree on. "What do you suggest?" he asks.

"Simon, do we have string?"

"Plenty," he replies. and hands me a bunch.

"If this enchanted place is breaking the rules. I say we

make up our own rules." I knot several pieces of string together and tie one end to an arrow.

"Flynn, what you are planning is impossible," says Simon.

I shoot the arrow high above the molten river, where it pierces the jagged stone ceiling. Holding the other end of the string, I say, "We will soon find out!" I look down at the flowing lava. If this doesn't work, I'll fall into that lava and be dead in seconds. I tug on the string, *I hope this holds*, and jump.

Spider web is called string in the game. Real string would break under the weight of a person, but digital string might as well be steel wire. It's very strong, however it doesn't last forever.

The distance between our wall and the other wall is far. As I swing across, I arc down, toward the lava. My path is like the swing on a swing set, each end is pretty high, but the middle is very low. I feel the heat coming up as I swing down, toward the fiery river. I start calculating, if the distance to this river is less than half of the distance to the other side . . . I'm doomed!

I should have thought this through better. A quick calculation and I would have recognized the problem before facing a scorching death! I'm nearly to the fire but my arc hasn't bottomed out yet. I'm going to hit the lava and burn! No, I can make it. I climb the rope in mid-swing, up a foot or two. I'm directly over the river now. I lift my legs, avoiding the lava. The end of the string drags in the river of lava and catches fire.

I'm on the upward arc now. Wow, that was close. Ouch! The fire is burning up the string and is scorching my feet. I pull farther up the rope. I'm nearing the far wall, getting closer to the once-distant passageway. The fire is burning the string, shortening it with each passing second. I imagine myself flying through the air and just missing the opening, hitting the sheer wall and sliding down into the magma below; I've got to let go at the right moment!

I let go, falling toward the opening. I'm so close, almost there. I reach forward but I'm falling too fast. The opening is too high. I can do this. I reach out. I miss the opening, thud. I hit the wall. But I'm not falling. I caught the lip of the ledge with my outstretched hand! Whew, I pull myself up.

"Yahoo!" I hear from the other side.

I'm safe in the new passageway. "Ok, your turn!" I yell back. I drop the string. It dangles. It doesn't have enough momentum to swing back to the other side.

"No way!" yells Enzo.

"Simon, you know what you have to do!" I yell.

Simon, quickly, robotically, mimics my earlier moves. He launches an arrow tied with string, it soars to the high stone ceiling. He grabs ahold of the string with one block hand and wraps his free block arm around Enzo. Simon has changed, grown, adapted. He handles stressful situations so much better than he did just a few days ago.

"Wait, what?" says Enzo, confused.

"Hold on," says Simon, as he jumps off the ledge,

taking Enzo with him.

"AAAAAAHHHH!" they both scream.

I watch in terror, they're too low: they need to climb up their string. They're going to swing into the lava!

Everything is in slow motion again. I tie string to two arrows; and launch one into the far wall and the other into the ceiling of the passageway where I stand. Moving at super digital speed, I zip along the tight line toward my swinging buddies. I'm moving at ten times the speed of my friends. I need to reach their string before they reach the lava below!

I reach their string and pull, raising them up a few feet. I hope I'm fast enough. They are inches from burning up!

I watch everything unfold before me. I've raised Simon high enough, but Enzo is lower, holding on to Simon's waist. Enzo will hit the lava if I don't do something. Even a slight touch of lava will set a player on fire.

It's too late. My super speed is not fast enough. Enzo's

legs drag through the lava.

"AHHHH," Enzo screams, it's slow motion for me.

They swing high and fast. Enzo is burning, holding tight to Simon who will soon be engulfed in flames too. They are high enough; Simon lets go of their string at the perfect moment, Enzo still holding tight to Simon's legs. They arc up, then down, landing in the opening. The darkness of the narrow pathway is now glowing with the fire of my burning friend.

I slide along my zip line toward my burning friend. What am I going to do? I don't know if stop, drop, and roll works if you're digital!

I jump from the zip line, fly-falling into the opening.

Cough, cough! I hear, who is that? Smoke everywhere, but there is no fire. It's dark.

"I was nearly burnt toast," coughs Enzo.

"Enzo! You're ok!? How?" I'm ecstatic!

"I doused him in water," replies Simon.

Enzo looks up at me and says. "Flynn. your movements are amazing. You've moved beyond super digital. You are now *ultra* digital."

I laugh as I help him up. "Whatever. you're just saying that to psyche me up to defeat Thorn. the *Ultra* Spider."

We made it, alive, to the other side! "Well. guys. the worst is over." I say as we turn to face the darkness.

LOG ENTRY 13

The Worst Is Over

DID I REALLY SAY, *THE WORST IS OVER*? I can't believe I used that cliché. In the movies, whenever anyone says that, the next thing that happens is worse! But this isn't a movie. This is real; we need to get out of this mountain so we can save the real world from digital destruction.

We wander for days in a labyrinth of tunnels. The path splits and splits again; we hit dead ends and find ourselves going in circles. We devise a system of marking our path by leaving torches inside each entryway, but even this is confusing. We come across torches that don't seem to be ours, or they are ours, but seem to have been moved. Simon and Enzo survive on health potions, because our food supply is gone.

"Flynn," says Simon, "how is your health status? Enzo

and I are getting low again. You haven't restored your health for days."

"Oh, I'm fine, Simon." I respond. Now that I consider this, it's true. I've watched as Simon and Enzo have restored their health recently, but my health status has remained fine. We move through passageways and Simon and Enzo always seem to lag behind. I'm in and out of dead ends before they have finished marking the entryway.

I'm changing, not my digital form, but my connection with the digital environment. I'm not sure how the transformation is occurring, but I'm not complaining.

"Guys, look at that blue glow." I say. "Let's follow that pathway."

They look at each other, then at me, confused. "What blue glow?" asks Simon.

"That . . ." I stop. "You don't see it?"

Enzo says, "We don't see any kind of light, other than

torchlight, Flynn."

"Follow me," I say. I follow the transparent blue fog-
like glow; it leads us through a random and confusing
path. We don't stop and explore every passage;
following the light saves time. I move smoothly,
quickly, the guys run to keep up.

"Do you feel that?" I ask, but I know better. They don't
feel the things I feel. I feel a sensation, the kind of
feeling I get in my stomach at the very top of a roller
coaster, just before starting back down. "Something is
near!"

I stop, waiting for the guys to catch up. We are at
another confusing intersection, but somehow I know the
way. I know something is just around the corner. I grab
my sword and whisper, "Get ready for battle, boys."

I jump around the corner, light! I see light, not the blue
glow we've been following. Daylight around the
corner! We rush ahead, and see the exit from this
demonic mountain! I'm so happy I could cry. I wish I
could let my emotions drain from my body now. Days

and days underground with no way out and unable to dig was almost too much.

Together, we walk through the exit. I look toward the sky and see the glow of the virtual sun. I close my eyes and imagine the warmth of the real sun, washing over me.

"We made it, we really made it." Enzo laughs, kind of a tense laugh. It sounds like he can't believe it. "Flynn, buddy, I will always trust your judgment in this game. I will follow you anywhere."

The mountain exit opens to a dense, green jungle. It's a beautiful sight. No mountains ahead. "I think that tunnel took us completely under the Treacherous Mountain range! I don't see another peak beyond this jungle."

Simon looks around, "Flynn, according to my calculations, we have traveled far enough to the west to be very near—"

"Hello, Flynn." Standing in the shade of the dense

jungle bush is a familiar face.

"Zana!" I hear myself yell with happiness. Sure, she creeps me out most of the time, but I'm still happy to see her.

"Where is your cat, Flynn?" she asks.

"We lost her at the entrance to the mountain," says Enzo.

"How did you know we'd be here?" I ask.

"Flynn, I am simply interested in seeing you fulfill your destiny."

"We could have used an interested party to guide us days ago," says Enzo with attitude. That's the same kind of thing I once said to Zana, but I've learned that she doesn't work that way. Simon looks skeptical, standing quietly.

"Do you know where you are, Flynn?" she asks. She takes a step toward us, but not into the light. She looks around, as she talks. "You should recognize this place."

I look at Simon. He stands silent. "Simon was about to tell us," I say. He looks away. A little irritated with Simon, I say, "I don't know, Zana, where are we?"

"You are very near where you first entered the digital world."

"You mean," I say, "Is this the jungle across the Clear Sea from Rescue Island? Is Citadel Fort near?" I'm excited! I look to the guys. I expect to see my excitement reflected in their faces.

Enzo's face is hard to read. His eyes narrow, one eyebrow raised. Simon is easy to read, he's uneasy. What do they sense that I don't? I'm the one with ultra digital powers! They must be jealous of my relationship with Zana.

"Yes, Flynn, beyond this jungle is Rescue Island, but your island is not why you are here, is it?" The way she asks questions makes me uncomfortable.

"Zana, we are here to do something important.

Something vital for the real world," I reply.

"Flynn, is this where you need to be in order to return to the physical world?" She asks. She doesn't like the term *real world*. Digital is real to her.

I know where she is going with her line of questions. It's always the same with her. She knows my destiny is to connect the physical and digital worlds, but she really doesn't know the details. "Zana, in order to fulfill my destiny," I watch her face light as I speak, "we first have to defeat Thorn." I don't want to tell Zana too much, I know the guys don't fully trust her. I also know that she doesn't know the details, so I can tell her that killing Thorn is necessary.

Her smile fades. I wait and let the words sink in. I look at Enzo; he looks mischievous. He recognizes my strategic manipulation of Zana and likes it. Simon, on the other hand, looks as if he's about to freak out.

"Flynn, that is impossible," says Zana. "I told you before, your weapons are no match for her."

"You said I'd have to outwit her. We can't do that without your help."

Zana looks at me, expressionless. What is she thinking? I hope she is considering helping us. Enzo spies a chicken, silently approaches it and kills it with his sword. He pockets the feathers and meat; he is not preparing for an end, he is preparing for a continuation. I love that his head is in the game. I wish I knew what he and Simon know. When and if we defeat Thorn, then what? Open the chest? Decode whatever we find inside? Find our way to Sage?

"If I help you, Flynn, you must promise that you will not leave the digital domain without me nearby." says Zana.

I consider her request. She is willing to help us defeat Thorn, the most dangerous creature in this place. and all she wants is to be nearby when I exit this place?

"We can't accept that." says Simon.

"Simon," I interrupt. "Let's not be hasty. No one is

more capable of defeating Thorn than Zana. We need more than weapons to defeat this spider. Zana can outwit Thorn."

"Slow down, Flynn." This time it's Enzo. "We need to talk in private."

"Excuse us, please, Zana," I say, a little bit irritated. We walk along the mountain, toward a bright clearing. Pop! It's Khan! "Where have you been?" I'm excited to see her. "You will be helpful soon enough," I say to her.

The enchantment of the mountain must have blocked her ability to appear near me. She's hungry, "Simon, I need raw fish." We walk into the jungle clearing. It's swampy here. Simon finds a small pond and catches several fish.

"Here you are, Flynn," he says as he gives me the fish. I feed Khan, who purrs and tries to pounce on me, but she is too fat for pouncing now. "Flynn," starts Enzo, "Simon and I do not trust Zana. We can't let her be with you when you exit the digital domain. That means she will learn of Sage. We can't let anyone discover Sage's hideaway. That's a terrible idea!"

"I agree with Enzo," says Simon. Big surprise.

"Guys, do you have a better idea to defeat Thorn? You've admitted it yourselves: we've all tried defeating her in the past, many times. How many times have we won? Exactly zero. I know you're putting a lot of faith in my ultra digital powers, and I appreciate that, but a huge asset just fell into our laps."

I continue, "Zana is the one who told me about Thorn. She said we must outwit her. If Zana knows how to outwit Thorn, we'd be crazy to not use her help. And what's the worst that can happen when we introduce her to Sage?"

Enzo looks at me with serious eyes and a grave voice. "You can't even imagine!"

LOG ENTRY 14

A Swarm of Spiders

ENZO'S THEATRICS ARE OVER. We all stand, somberly.

"Ok, we'll do it without Zana. As a team, we will battle Thorn, the three of us and Khan." That was very hard to say. The words did not want to come out. I respect these guys, and I trust them. They know much that I don't know, and I believe they are making the best choice they can. "I'll tell Zana."

As I return to Zana, I think about battling Thorn without her. I get anxious anytime I am near Thorn. That spider makes me nervous; she is smarter than me. For all I know she is watching us right now.

I imagine what happens in Thorn's head. I imagine what she sees as she looks at us from her hiding place;

her vision is focused on darkness and blood. Everything is dark, then she sees us; we are blood red. Her killer instincts take over. But she doesn't attack directly. She takes her time, strategizing. She hides in the shadows, ensuring the safety of her hidden chest and protecting her lair.

With that unnerving image in mind, I wonder how we avoid walking into a trap. Do we stay together or split up?

There is strength in numbers, but if we split up maybe one of us will reach the chest while Thorn battles the others. However, Thorn is great at attacking one-on-one, and this way we could lose. She definitely has the advantage.

I reach the edge of the jungle where we left Zana. I don't see Zana. I enter the jungle; it's light enough to see in here, even though no direct sunlight penetrates the green canopy above.

"Zana, can we talk?" No response. I walk in farther. Where is she? The further in I go, the darker it gets.

Plod, crunch, plod, crunch; here comes Khan, panting, crushing everything she steps on. Having a cat near makes me feel safe. "Zana!"

I sense impending doom.

Slurp, slurp, slurp! I've walked into a trap! I wish Verve were here! I turn around to see brown spiders and blue spiders descending from the trees and creeping up from the brush and every dark hiding place. I'm in trouble.

I enter ultra digital mode. Arrows fly, sluip-ahhh, killing one, then two, spiders. Something falls from above, and without looking up I swap my bow for my sword and slice, thud, poof. A cave spider disappears, dead. What are cave spiders doing in the jungle?

The attack accelerates, two at a time, then four, then ten. I'm spinning, slicing, moving at extreme speed. Thud, sluip, thud, poof. I need help! I spin quickly with my sword out; I feel like a blender, chopping everything that comes near me.

Slicing, I look around; the jungle is dark with poisonous

eyes. I don't see what I expect to see: I'm looking for Thorn, a seven-legged spider. She'll remember me: I'm the one who took one of her legs in our last battle. I certainly remember her. Her bite is more deadly than anything I've faced.

The jungle grows suddenly darker. The tingling feeling grows stronger. Screech! I look up. The darkness is falling from above! It's Thorn! Somehow she planned this, organized the spiders to keep me busy in defensive mode. She's been watching and found my weakness. I can't defend above and around me at the same time: they're coming too fast. She is dropping quickly, but she is not the same spider I last saw. She has been modified! Her stubby leg, the one I cut off, has been replaced with an iron leg, sharpened at the end. Her bite isn't the only danger she possesses: that sharp, steel leg is a weapon!

What to do? Plan A: keep spinning and take out the growing mass of spiders coming from all sides. Terrible plan; Thorn will plant her sharp spike in my head from above. Plan B: direct my efforts above, to Thorn. The absolute mass of spiders surrounding me will crush me while I battle the arachnid above.

I've done it before, and I do it again. Plan C: I redirect my sword, pointing it down, away from Thorn. I have exactly enough time to dig two blocks down before I'm spiked, crushed, and poisoned. I'm safe! Now I only have to defend upward; spiders can't come down a hole this small. I look up the moment before Thorn would have planted her spike in my skull. She stands directly above me, her face angry.

Thwapp, she is knocked to the side; thwapp, another arrow sinks into her side. Thwapp, thwapp, they are coming fast. I swing at her from my hole, but she was knocked too far away by the bombardment of arrows. She retreats, disappearing into the mass of spiders.

"It's about time!" I yell out of the hole. Simon and Enzo finally decided to check on me. They expected me to be talking with Zana, not fighting an army of spiders.

Forget fighting these spiders, there are too many! I dig down another block and then tunnel toward my friends.

Every so often I dig up to the surface to look around and get a feel for where I am. A minute later I open up near my friends.

"Guys, is it safe to come up?"

"No!" screams Simon. It seems the spider army turned on them. I dig a hole under Enzo. then Simon. They fall down to my level. Khan plops down with us.

"It's safer down here. Spiders can't fit through single block openings." I yell.

Ahh! A cave spider has bitten me: I see red and yellow. pain and poison. What's a cave spider doing in the tunnel?

Slash, poof. Simon makes quick work of two spiders. Then, moving quickly, he fills the openings above.

"You forgot about cave spiders. they can fit in small spaces," chuckles Enzo.

We are closed in. Simon plants torches on the walls and returns to me with a healing potion. But I don't need it.

I'm healing rapidly.

"Looks like you had a nice chat with Zana," jokes Enzo. I love how he can make light of a near-death experience.

"She was gone. When I looked for her, I was ambushed by that venomous army above."

"Flynn, it is highly probable that Zana is involved in the ambush," says Simon.

"It's highly probable that you're being a jerk. Of course she didn't set that up. She was going to help us kill Thorn. Why would she help Thorn with an ambush? Besides, she said that she needs me to fulfill my destiny. She needs me to survive," I say angrily.

"It's ironic that we are back in the ground after trying to get out of that mountain for days," Enzo says with a smile.

I look at his smile, my irritation toward Simon fades and I laugh. We all laugh. Simon's laugh sounds like a nervous child, but that's just me being mean.

"Did you guys see the iron leg on Thorn?" I ask.

"I knew that was the Ultra Spider after seeing her brilliant attack," says Enzo. "What's with the shiny leg?"

"Remember when I told you that I cut one of her legs off? You said it would become a weakness, but it seems it actually became a strength. That thing could've put holes in me," I say.

"I remember. I had no idea a mob could regenerate with an upgrade. I'm glad you didn't cut all of her legs off or we'd be in real trouble." Enzo and I laugh at this. Simon smiles.

"Thorn is a modified spider; if only her spider bite would give me Spider-Man powers." I joke. "I don't think her metal leg is a regeneration. Something or someone is responsible for that spiked leg."

Simon looks serious, "We need a plan."

"Ok. Good idea," I say, "Thorn is guarding a crate, somewhere in the jungle near Spider Sands." I'm proud to show the guys my map of Rescue Island and the surrounding area. "The crate contains something important, but we don't know what."

Enzo is irritated, "Stop calling it a crate! It's a chest, not a crate."

I guess I pushed one of his buttons. "Whatever. The point is, we need a failsafe plan to get the contents of the cra—, er, chest."

"Based on an analysis of previous battles with the spider, our probability of a victorious three-way attack is less than 2 percent," says Simon.

"Don't ever tell me the odds!" Enzo and I both yell, quoting Han Solo.

"Someone please point out the lair on my map," I say. "I've never actually seen it." Enzo smiles at me. I can't tell if he's thinking of a joke or laughing at me making a plan without knowing where we are attacking.

"It's here," Simon points to the map. He points to the eastern edge of the map, on the south end of Spider Sands, near the jungle.

"Where is the chest?" I ask.

Simon replies, "The spider's lair is a cave, and the chest is deep inside."

"So, what's the plan?" asks Enzo. "How are we going to get to that chest?"

"I have an idea," I say, " but we need to get moving before it gets dark." I tunnel in the direction of the water. We're under the jungle now. Tunneling goes quickly, it's mostly dirt and sand. Reaching cobblestone, we stop. We build stairs up and out. Our exit is near a small, stone mound, on the edge of Spider Sands near the jungle. I look west and see a beautiful sight. The sun is in the western sky, showing Citadel Fort in a scenic silhouette.

"Beautiful castle, man," says Enzo. "Not really your style, though."

"I built it for safety."

"I certainly looks secure," says Simon. "Flynn, you've been battling with that sword for too long. Here, have a new one," he holds a sword out for me.

I check the damage level of my sword. "Simon, I don't need a new sword. Mine shows no damage." I check my other tools, "none of my tools show damage, Simon." This is awesome!

We are in the open, not far from the sandy beach where I first woke up in the game, face down in the sand. It seems so long ago. We are south of a stone mound, covered by jungle plants.

Simon whispers, "That mound is Thorn's lair. The entrance is on the other side. We need to go into the jungle to enter her lair."

"Do we?" I ask, "Or is there another way?"

"Flynn, we've tried getting to the chest many times," says Simon, "Every time, we go through that entrance.

How else would we enter?"

"Now you're asking the right question." I reply.

LOG ENTRY 15

Thorn's Stand

"THORN COULD BE ALMOST ANYWHERE," I say. "What we know is that she tends to stay in dark, shadowy places. We also know that she is aware of us. She will be watching for us and she has likely set a trap for us."

"And what's the good news?" laughs Enzo.

I look at him and say, "The good news is that we are not going through the front door."

It's quiet for a moment while Enzo and Simon look quizzically at each other. Enzo looks at me and says, "Flynn, I'm afraid your memory is failing you. Simon and I know this place very well, and there is only one entrance."

"Yes, Flynn," Simon says, enforcing Enzo's statement,

"We have tried everything. When we sent the protocol ocelot, Verve, to spy, she confirmed it. There is only one way in and one way out."

"We need to consider options deeper than the ones in front of us. And by deeper. I mean digging deep." I pull a shovel from my pocket.

Enzo looks at me with a mischievous smile. "I see where you are going."

"Simon," I say, "I need coordinates for the chest. from the end point of our tunnel."

"It's twenty-four blocks north and six blocks east. why?" says Simon.

"Follow me," I enter our tunnel. walk six blocks east. then start digging north.

"Oh, Flynn, this is brilliant." says Simon.

"We are going to come up directly under the chest. If we're lucky, we'll avoid Thorn completely." I'm pretty proud of the plan.

We're digging through stone. We move as fast as we can expect and in a short time we reach Simon's coordinates. "Ok, guys, assuming nothing has changed, two blocks above us is the chest that contains the secrets to the digital crisis that is sweeping over the real world."

I dig upward, hoping to expose the wooden bottom of a chest. Crr, crr, crr, thud, thud, thud. I stop. I broke through and hit obsidian.

"That's it," says Simon. "It's an indestructible chest made from obsidian."

We are standing under the chest. This is an intense moment. We have reached the chest, never before have we been this close. We are moments away from discovering the truth about the digital crisis!

"Open it," says Enzo.

Normally chests can be accessed from any side. Access to the contents doesn't require standing above the chest.

By tapping a chest the contents appear as an inventory grid. I try. It doesn't open. "It's locked." I say.

"We knew there would be trouble. you said something about using your algorithm to break the lock code." says Enzo.

"That was when I knew the algorithm." I say. "I have a better idea. Simon, give me as much TNT as you have!"

"I have fifty-nine blocks." he replies.

"It's a figure of speech. Give me eight blocks." I stack the explosive into a cube. two wide. two deep and two high, directly below the chest. I light it with flint and steel, sssss. "RUN!!!"

Enzo is first. followed by Simon and me. We make it to the main tunnel and hide around the corner.

Boom! BOOOM!!!

I feel the explosions in my body. Wow! The others are momentarily stunned. I return to the pathway and what I see is amazing. Daylight. The explosion left a crater in the ground and opened the ceiling to daylight. I walk down the pathway. Everything is blown away. No spider lair, no chest, just a giant hole in the ground. I notice my ears ringing from the explosion.

"Guys, we have a problem!" I yell. "I don't know where the contents of the chest are!"

Simon and Enzo come around the corner. Their eyes are wide.

"What have you done?" asks Enzo.

I don't reply. It's obvious. I blew everything to bits.

Simon looks concerned, and says, "It appears we used too much explosive."

I climb down, into the pit. I look around. Above is the canopy of the jungle. To the east the jungle is thick and dark. To the west the sky opens on Spider Sands, Rescue Island, and the setting sun.

I look around, slowly, scanning everything in sight. I have no idea what I'm looking for, but I have a feeling that I'll know it when I see it.

"What happens now? What do we do? We have no idea what was in the box, what it means, or what to do now that it's blown to bits." whines Simon.

Enzo is angry, "AHHHH! What now? How could we be so dumb!" he yells. At least he's not blaming me.

The sun is a sliver on the western horizon. "Guys, we don't have time for this," I say, still surveying the scene.

"Don't have time! We just blew up any hope of saving the world from the digital crisis!" Now Enzo *is* mad at me. "Don't tell me what we have time for!"

I see the lid of the chest, fully intact lying next to the main box. It looks nearly perfect. Near that, I see something, a tiny glowing blue sphere in the jungle, at the edge of the crater. I run toward it as daylight turns to dusk.

"Don't run away from me, we haven't finished this

conversation," I hear Enzo's angry words behind me.

It's dark under the canopy; I'm halfway to the glowing sphere when I sense impending doom. The explosion alerted the creatures of the night. My sword slices, thwapp, thwing. I deflect arrows.

"Guys, we have visitors!" I yell, hoping the guys will set aside their anger long enough to give me a hand. I let arrows fly, groan, sluip, hiss, thud. Creatures fall, I slip into ultra mode.

The battle distracts me for a few moments. I turn to the glowing sphere, but it's gone!

"Any time now, guys!" I scream, as I charge toward the last place I saw the sphere. Slice, groan, SSSSS! Thwapp, thud, thud. I switch between my sword and bow in a single motion. Slice, three zombies fall, poof. Thwapp, my arrow finds a pixelator, poof. I'm almost there. Where is that sphere? "Guys!" They can't be holding a grudge in a situation like this, can they?

I turn to my buddies and discover why they aren't with

me. Simon is battling a mass of spiders and Enzo is wrapped in web, trapped!

I rush to my friends. "Stop!" yells Enzo. "It's a trap! Don't trust—"

Just then, a shiny, silver spike pokes through Enzo's chest from behind. Thorn's spiked leg!

Poof! Enzo is gone.

"NOOOOO!" I yell. I see red. I can't control my anger. I rush Thorn, slicing through the army of spiders separating us.

Sluip, thud, poof. My movements are clear, my anger fogs my vision, but my body moves on its own. Each swing of my sword takes out a dozen spiders. I feel the ultra powers within, moving me forward, toward my enemy.

Thorn looks at me, she smiles at what she's done. I rush her, swinging my sword left to right, targeting her head.

Clink! She blocks my sword with her iron leg.

"AHHHH!" I scream, as I swing again. Again she blocks my attack. I lunge at her, stabbing, she dodges my sword and brings her spike down on top of me. I let my anger take me into her kill zone! I'm in serious trouble. What was I thinking?

I block her spike, but not her bite. I see red; I'm on the ground, under her. I slice through one of her legs, and it falls to the ground. Screech! She is angry. As I roll, I hear a metallic thud and feel pain. "AHHHH!" her spike pins my sword arm to the ground. I lie on my back, face-to-face with death. My skin glows red, reflecting the radiance of her eyes.

I hear a scream, "AHHHH, I'm sorry, Flynn. We failed!" It's Simon. Thud, he falls to the ground. In a moment it will all be over.

The red haze of my vision fades. I feel calmness overcome me. I see it! The blue glow of the sphere is coming from behind Thorn; she is protecting it.

I do the only thing I can think to do in this situation; I punch Thorn in the face with my free hand. Screech!

She leans back, and while keeping her spiked leg in my sword-wielding arm, pins my legs and arms with her many legs. I recognize the look on her face. She is going to poison me. AHHHH! I see a bright light.

Shlop! Everything stops. The pain stops. the biting stops. Thorn falls to the side. Her spiked leg still in my arm tips over. I'm no longer pinned to the ground. The brightness fades, and as it fades I see the silhouette of a figure holding a sword. The sword penetrating Thorn's skull from above. The sound of battle grows silent. I hear the scuttling feet of creatures. retreating to the jungle.

I look at the silhouette. darkness returning to my vision. A splash potion reverses the effects of the poison. It's a zombie, standing above me. holding the sword that killed Thorn. It's Zana!

Poof! Thorn disappears. leaving behind only the spike of her leg. lodged in my arm. I pull the spike out of my arm and stand up. slowly. Simon is lying in the pit. I run to him. Sitting next to him I say. "Simon. Simon.

look at me."

"I've never felt so awful," he says, sadly. I can't tell if he feels bad from battle wounds or from the loss of Enzo.

"You made it! I'm so happy you made it!" I say.

I stand up and help Simon to his feet. We turn to Zana. "Zana, I don't know how to thank you. I would be dead now, if you hadn't killed Thorn."

Simon looks down and says, "Zana, I must confess, I haven't trusted you." He looks up, looks Zana in the eyes, "But I do now. Thank you for saving us from a gruesome death."

I look to the only evidence of Thorn's defeat, her iron leg. "Where is the blue sphere?" I ask, "It was there, with the spider. I saw it when Thorn disappeared."

"Flynn. I have the egg," says Zana. "Is that why you are here, Flynn, for the egg?"

"Yes," I reply. "That egg holds the key to something

important in the physical world. Zana. Please give it to me."

Zana replies, "Flynn. I'll keep it safe. You can trust me."

LOG ENTRY 16

Introduce the Unexpected

SIMON IS VISIBLY UPSET, "I can't believe we lost Enzo," he sobs. He's taking it really hard.

"I know, buddy, but he didn't really die. He's out there, just not with us here anymore," I say to comfort him. "I do wish he was with us, though."

I look around. It's surprisingly quiet for nighttime in a jungle. "Let's cross Clear Sea to Rescue Island. It's a safe place to stay until daylight."

Zana's face turns toward me, "Flynn, we will not travel during the daylight. That is not safe for me. We will travel at night, and now is the perfect time to start."

"We?" queries Simon.

Zana looks squarely at Simon, and says, "I am going

with you, to keep the egg safe. I will not leave your side until Flynn safely fulfills his destiny."

An egg is the perfect container for code. Simon doesn't see the blue glow; I'm not sure whether Zana does. I don't want to bring it up with her, since the last time I told her about my senses she gave me a creepy stare and brushed it aside.

"You are both strong warriors," says Zana.

I nod. Simon thanks her, meekly. His courage in battle does not match his timid personality.

Zana looks around the area, surveying the crater left by the explosion. "What happened here?"

Simon replies, "We had a plan to open the chest protected by the spider. We used TNT." Simon's speech is intelligent around me, but clumsy around Zana.

"It worked, too," I say. "I don't like the giant hole here. This was a beautiful place. Scary, but beautiful."

"Why did you choose to blow up the chest?" Zana asks.

"It was locked," Simon sounds proud of himself for having an answer.

Zana looks skeptical. That answer isn't convincing enough. She asks, "How did you know explosives would work?"

"It was Flynn's idea," says Simon. He looks down, as if he's embarrassed for not knowing more of the answer.

"Simple," I say, "Coders can't plan for everything. I thought of all the things I'd defend against. I'd lock it with an encrypted code. I'd secure the location. I'd install a defense network. And, just to be safe, instead of constructing it out of wood, I'd make it out of something indestructible, like obsidian."

Continuing, I say, "The last thing on my list would be protecting it against something as crazy as TNT. Every gamer knows that to break a chest you just whack on it. A programmer writing protection code for a chest would protect it from the impact of tools. Anyone trying to get to the valuable contents of that chest would be afraid to use explosives. They would be afraid of the harm it would do to the contents."

"Why did the explosives blow up the box but not the contents, Flynn?" Zana says. It sounds like she is challenging me.

"The person who coded that chest overlooked the weakest component. The weakest link was the hinge point. I didn't know it at the time. but I had hoped for the a glitch in the hinge. and it worked."

"And why didn't it blow up the contents?" Zana queries.

"I didn't believe that whatever was in there was subject to game rules. so it wouldn't break in an explosion. The egg isn't an egg at all. It's a shell that contains some kind of code. It's brilliant!" I laugh.

Simon is somber, not ready to laugh with me. I realize that I'm being insensitive. so I stop laughing.

"Simon, can we talk?" I ask. He looks at me. "We need

to take this egg to Sage. I don't know what to do with it; I hope Sage will."

Simon looks away, as if pondering. He knows I'm right. "Flynn, you don't have the access code required to see Sage, but I do. You are asking me to break a vow I made to you by taking you and Zana to the secret and secure location of Sage. Your request will expose the spawn point of the Hackers and me. But the most dangerous thing you are asking me to do is to introduce two unauthorized, intelligent beings to the sacred place that houses the brain activity port. The place that connects the digital world with the real world."

Simon stops for a moment and looks at Zana, then back at me. "The place we must travel to is protected by a strong security system. It's hidden and it has a defense network. It's virtually indestructible." He looks directly into my eyes, "Flynn, what you are asking me to do is exactly what you did to the spider's lair. You are asking me to introduce the unexpected. This is unplanned and we cannot know what will happen."

"Flynn," says Simon, "Have I missed something?

Surely this is not what you are asking me to do?"

I look at Zana, then at Simon, and say, "That is exactly what I am asking you to do!"

THANKS FOR READING!

WHAT HAPPENS NEXT? Find out in Flynn's Log 3: The Ultimate Form of Life. Get your copy here:

StoneMarshall.com/flynns-log-3/

I love my readers, I couldn't do this without you! Word-of-mouth is crucial for any author to succeed. If you enjoyed the book, please consider leaving a review. Even if it's only a line or two, it would be a huge help.

StoneMarshall.com/flynns-log-2-review

Thank you

THE SERIES: FLYNN'S LOG

In the near future, video games begin to change and evolve. Random bits of data create a virtual intelligence that takes over the digital world. A digital crisis is born, bringing the real world to a halt. The only person who can save the world is Flynn, but he needs help from his friends, the Hackers.

Flynn's Log 1: Rescue Island

The world is in trouble and needs a hacker hero.

Flynn, a hacker, enters a familiar but changing video game world where something goes terribly wrong.

Flynn gets stuck inside the game! His memory is lost and the dangers he faces are real. The game world evolves introducing new dangers and creatures that Flynn has never seen before. An intelligent creature comes to his aid, but can Flynn trust this digital being?

StoneMarshall.com/Flynns-log-1

Flynn's Log 2: Thorn's Lair

Stuck in a video game and facing certain death, Flynn takes his only option. He steps through a portal. . .

Flynn and friends travel into a terrifying place and face never before seen masses of mobs! Flynn discovers why he is in the game and learns how to exit, but it will not be easy.

To fulfill his destiny he must make a dangerous journey. With the help of his friends both digital and physical, will Flynn get out?

StoneMarshall.com/flynns-log2

Flynn's Log 3: The Ultimate Form of Life

Flynn must fulfill his destiny and connect the digital and physical worlds!

Stuck inside the digital game-world. Flynn faces a true crisis; what is real? Is his ultra-digital body more real than his physical body? What would it be like to stay in the digital world forever?

StoneMarshall.com/flynns-log-3

Flynn's Log 4

To Be Continued . . .

StoneMarshall.com/flynns-log4

Other books by Stone Marshall:

StoneMarshall.com/titles

THE STONE MARSHALL CLUB

Join the Stone Marshall Club and get freebies, fun stuff and exclusive content.

StoneMarshall.com/club

- Freebies: Graphics and wallpaper for your device

- State of Stone: Author notes and Development diary

- Intelligence: Character information from Flynn's world

- Get news and updates by email so you'll never miss an update or book release.

Join Now! Membership is fun, easy and free.

ABOUT THE AUTHOR

STONE MARSHALL likes comics, games, running, the Ramones, and travel.

Stone reads stories with his son at bedtime. Sometimes, when they finish a book before falling asleep, Stone fills the time by creating great stories starring his son, Nabru. It is a wonderful time to share lessons about life and relationships.

In turn, Nabru becomes involved in the incredible adventures, adding his thoughts and perspectives. The ideas and stories of Nabru are the seeds of the amazing books that have become this series.

Made in the USA
Lexington, KY
15 November 2016